CUTTING EDGE

NEW STORIES OF MYSTERY AND CRIME BY WOMEN WRITERS

Laurel Hausler

EDITED BY **JOYCE CAROL OATES**

BROOKLYN, NEW YORK, USA
BALLYDEHOB, CO. CORK, IRELAND

Published by Akashic Books
©2019 The Ontario Review Inc.

"Please Translate" by Edwidge Danticat was originally published in an earlier form in the Fall 2014 issue of *Conjunctions* magazine; the Margaret Atwood poems "Thriller Suite" and "Update on Werewolves" were originally published on Wattpad.

Cover and interior artwork by Laurel Hausler

Hardcover ISBN: 978-1-61775-761-7
Paperback ISBN: 978-1-61775-762-4
Library of Congress Control Number: 2019935265

Akashic Books
Brooklyn, New York, USA
Ballydehob, Co. Cork, Ireland
Twitter: @AkashicBooks
Facebook: AkashicBooks
E-mail: info@akashicbooks.com
Website: www.akashicbooks.com

Table of Contents

Introduction // 5

Part I: Their Bodies, Our Selves
One of These Nights by Livia Llewellyn // 17
A History of the World in Five Objects by S.J. Rozan // 33
The Hunger by Lisa Lim // 39
Too Many Lunatics by Lucy Taylor // 54
Please Translate by Edwidge Danticat // 69

Part II: A Doom of One's Own
The Boy without a Bike by Jennifer Morales // 79
An Early Specimen by Elizabeth McCracken // 96
OBF, Inc. by Bernice L. McFadden // 108
Firetown by Aimee Bender // 121
Thief by Steph Cha // 135

Part III: Manslaying
Impala by S.A. Solomon // 147
Mothers, We Dream by Cassandra Khaw // 160
Il Grifone by Valerie Martin // 173
Miss Martin by Sheila Kohler // 197
Six Poems by Margaret Atwood // 214
Assassin by Joyce Carol Oates // 226

About the Contributors // 236

Introduction

Female Noir

In the old days, all werewolves were male.
—Margaret Atwood

I s there a distinctive female noir? Is there, as some have argued, a distinctive female voice, differing essentially from the male voice? Neuroanatomists have revealed that the female and male brains of *Homo sapiens* differ significantly, though not in ways that clearly pinpoint distinctive behavior, and without reference to superior intelligence, talent, or traits of personality. In other words, there are neuroanatomical differences in female and male beings, as there are obvious physiological differences between the sexes, but these differences are modulated by countless other factors—genetic inheritance, familial upbringing, education, culture, environment.

It has been noted that noir isn't a specific subject matter but rather a sort of (dark) music: a sensibility, a tone, an atmosphere. The stark, stoic melancholy of Edward Hopper's *Nighthawks*. Solitary, shadowed objects in the paintings of de Chirico. Not the bland, flat surfaces of sunshine but the tonal drama of chiaroscuro. The music of Robert Johnson, Billie Holiday, Lena Horne, Nina Simone. Miles Davis's soundtrack for the French film *Elevator to the Gallows*. Dark eroticism of the poetry of Sylvia Plath fusing desire, sexual rage, unspeakable longing. "Emotions on wet roads on autumn nights" (Wallace Stevens). The very titles *Touch of Evil; Farewell, My Lovely; A Kiss Before Dying;* "Kiss Me Again, Stranger." Not so much pessimistic as starkly realist, free of romantic illusion, expecting the less benign, resigned to the worst. Noir is a populist sort of tragic vision, making of a man's infatuation with a woman, in traditional noir, something richly ironic, and often lethal—not profound, as in classic tragedy, but a confirmation of the way the (actual) world is: deceptive, punishing. Noir is frequently, though not inevitably, romantic/sexual disillusion, fury. The dying words of Hemingway's Harry Morgan in *To Have and Have Not* are sheer noir, despair raised to the level of wisdom: ". . . a man alone ain't got no bloody chance."

As for a *woman* alone, Hemingway is silent. In noir, women's place until fairly recently has been limited to two: muse, sexual object. As Edgar Allan Poe noted, "The death of a beautiful woman is, unquestionably, the most poetical topic in the world."

Honoré de Balzac remarked that behind every great fortune there is a crime. Certainly, behind most great works of literature there is a crime, or crimes—the rich, fecund soil in which noir flourishes. In our present-day American republic, in an era of scarcely concealed public corruption and unrepentant scandal, noir seems to have spread like minuscule drops of anthrax in a reservoir.

What is distinctive about female noir isn't likely to be an identifiable prose style, nor even a prevailing sensibility, but rather perspective: where the noir tradition in American fiction and films has been predominantly male, our perspective has been *male-directed*; in female noir, we are allowed to see, with a good deal of individual variation, from the point of view of the female observer, actor, agent. Suddenly, the *male* becomes the object of the protagonist's gaze, which happens to be *female*. (Though some female observers in *Cutting Edge* apprehend *female* from the perspective of the lesbian gaze, as in Aimee Bender's homage to Raymond Chandler/LA noir in her teasingly erotic "Firetown." In Jennifer Morales's "The Boy without a Bike," the lesbian perspective, which doesn't shy away from a confrontation with [male] physical violence, comes to include the tenderly maternal and protective as well.)

What has long been an accepted cultural phenomenon, as embedded in the natural order of things as the physical body itself, is revealed by the female gaze as culturally determined, and therefore mutable. It's true, the great works of American noir have primarily been by men—from Chandler's *The Big Sleep* and *Farewell, My Lovely,* Hammett's *The Maltese Falcon* and *Red Harvest,* James M. Cain's *The Postman Always Rings Twice,* to such film classics as *Double Indemnity, Out of the Past, They Drive By Night, They Live By Night, Laura, Vertigo,* and countless more, encoding the femme fatale as the driving force of evil; even works of mystery and detection by women writers (Agatha Christie, P.D. James, Ruth Rendell) continued the tradition of the brilliant (if flawed) male detective. Angela Carter's radical interpretation of the fairy tale, *The Bloody Chamber* (1979), marked a dramatic turn in literary fiction, in Carter's ecstatic celebration of the very evil of the female, where once such energies had been the unique property of the male. Though there had been evil female characters previously in literature, from murderous Medea and Clytemnestra to savage Goneril and Regan and (more recently) insufferable little Rhoda Penmark of William March's *The Bad Seed* and the more piteous psycho-murderer Merricat Blackwood of Shirley Jackson's *We Have Always Lived in the Castle*, it is in the second half of the twentieth century, with the rise of feminism, that the female vision, in its appropriation of the energies of male evil, is in itself celebrated.

As the inscrutable narrator of Valerie Martin's "Il Grifone" boasts: "Murder is my métier . . . I made my living spinning plots."

If the werewolf has been a cultural archetype embodying man's animal nature in its most obvious, literal manifestation, it is also the case that, until recent times, as Margaret Atwood observes in her poem "Update on Werewolves," the werewolf was perceived to be an exaggeration of *maleness*. To be female was to be "feminine"—passively vulnerable to harassment and victimization by men; "femininity" could not be equated with a murderous animal nature. (By literary tradition, vampires could be either male or female: Count Dracula is the vampire patriarch, but he has several vampire-wives who are eager to do his bidding and infect men with the vampire curse; Joseph Sheridan Le Fanu's *Carmilla,* which in fact predated Bram Stoker's *Dracula* by twenty-six years, introduces a highly erotic, seductive female/lesbian vampire who never repents her evil behavior.)

Gender divisions in art are futile to debate, though there is a common-sense likelihood that subject matter is often more clearly aligned with one sex than the other, if one acknowledges the binary nature of sex. (In our time, in some quarters, biological identity at birth is no longer considered permanently binding: one can "transcend" one's birthright.) Childbirth, nursing, the travails and ecstasies of inhabiting a female body, experiences of sexual harassment, abuse, exploitation—these are likely to be female subjects, of course; yet, the great American photographer Margaret Bourke-White ventured into such pits of horror as the Buchenwald concentration camp to take photographs for *Life* at the end of World War II, an assignment that few male photographers might have been capable of undertaking; and the contemporary Norwegian author Karl Ove Knausgård, in his six-volume autobiographical novel *My Struggle,* tracks the domestic life of a father with young children in its exhaustive domestic particularities as few women/mothers would have the patience to do. These extremes may be anomalies but they certainly challenge the conventional patriarchal wisdom that "anatomy is destiny"—still more, that "a woman's place is in the home"—or Robert Graves's churlish remark, ". . . woman is not a poet: she is either a Muse or she is nothing."

It is a curiosity that "mystery" is usually associated with crime, and crime invariably with murder, when in fact mysteries abound in our lives that may have nothing to do with crime, nor even with physical distress. So, too, noir may be about subjects other than crime; yet in literature and film it is invariably associated with crimes, usually murder; in classic noir, the crime (murder) springs from a male protagonist having been tangled in a web spun by a femme fatale, herself heartless. The femme fatale inspires desire in the male but is herself immune to such weakness, which makes her a monstrous being, usually in proximity to a "good" woman— Marilyn Monroe in *Niagara,* the brazen platinum-blond beauty in contrast to the unspectacular young wife played by brunette Jean Peters; Kim Novak in *Vertigo*, a platinum-blond enigma in contrast to the plain, mousy "good girl" artist played by Barbara Bel Geddes. It's significant that the Hollywood noir film that most realistically (and sympathetically) explores the consequence of sexual violence against women is Ida Lupino's *Outrage*, a portrait of a young woman rape victim in which there isn't the slightest suggestion of blaming the victim or suggesting any sort of complicity with the rapist. *Outrage* evokes genuine terror as the victim is stalked by her rapist in a German expressionist cityscape which traps her as in a maze, and explores with remarkable subtlety and candor the struggle of the young woman to regain autonomy over her shattered personality. Here is a noir film in which the female protagonist emerges as the heroine of her own life—a film so far ahead of its time, it remains relatively unknown to this day.

More frequently, films in which women are sexual victims have been carefully contrived revenge dramas in which a heroic male protagonist, likely to be a husband or lover, reverts to vigilante justice after a girl or a woman has suffered violence; the female is the narrative pretext for the male struggle with another male, or males, for dominance. From *The Searchers* to *Death Wish*, from *Straw Dogs* to *Memento*, this cinematic category is inexhaustible, and contains much that is excellent as well as much that is cheaply exploitative. What the revenge films have in common is the enraged male perspective, which justifies whatever violence is unleashed.

The particular strength of the female noir vision isn't a recognizable style but rather a defiantly female, indeed feminist, perspective. *Cutting Edge* brings together a considerable range of twenty-first-century female voices, from sociological realism (Cha) to Grand Guignol surrealism (Oates); from erotic playfulness (Bender) to dark fairy-tale determinism (Khaw). Here is a brilliantly deadpan graphic story by Lisa Lim, and here are brilliantly executed poems by Margaret Atwood. Artwork by Laurel Hausler is striking and original, sinister and triumphant; *Noir Dame* (on the front cover) is the perfect image of a mysterious beauty, far more than merely skin-deep, and essentially unknowable.

As one might expect, a number of these stories wreak vengeance upon the opposite sex. The adolescent protagonist of S.A. Solomon's "Impala" is a victim of sexual abuse by a high school boyfriend/gang leader from whom she must flee to save her life; in a narrative of steadily mounting suspense, she confronts the prospect of further violence from a stranger encountered on her runaway flight. The mystery-writer protagonist of Valerie Martin's "Il Grifone" is threatened by a brute ("Half eagle, half lion; on the ground, in the air, all predator, all the time") whom other men, including her husband, can't seem to take seriously, even as the reader identifies strongly with her predicament, and thrills to the ingenious way she eludes what might have been a sordid fate: "I'm much less likely to commit a crime because I've thought about all the ways it can go wrong . . ." Martin is particularly adroit at presenting the maddening complicity of men with men— the assumption that a threatened woman is imagining things, even on the part of "sympathetic" men.

In the structurally inventive "A History of the World in Five Objects," S.J. Rozan tracks the ritualistic behavior of a woman who has survived a traumatizing childhood only to be confronted with the ruins of her personality as an adult.

In an artful variation on the theme of revenge, Steph Cha's "Thief" dramatizes a domestic, familial quandary in which tragic loss and betrayal yield to a kind of forgiveness; of necessity, an older generation yields to a younger, for whom life in Koreatown is fraught with more danger than the narrowly virtuous law-abiding elders can imagine.

"Death always made her hungry" is the heart of Lisa Lim's deftly narrated graphic tale "The Hunger"—a thoroughly unrepentant revenge against another sort of enemy, one within the family. Lucy Taylor's conversational, confiding "Too Many Lunatics" and Livia Llewellyn's coolly narrated "One of These Nights" present deceptively reasonable, ostensibly sympathetic female characters who are revealed as more complex than the reader has suspected: in "Too Many Lunatics," a half sister is determined to save her addict-sister from harm, with unanticipated consequences for both of them; in "One of These Nights," the sinister alliance between two teenage girls and the father of one of them is only gradually revealed, with unanticipated consequences for a third girl. Edwidge Danticat's "Please Translate" is a small masterpiece of suspense that has its roots in the classic noir situation in which a woman and a man are locked in mortal combat over the (literal) body of their child, a hostage to adult infidelity and selfishness; in "The Boy without a Bike," a concerned woman dares to monitor the behavior of a possibly abusive father, imperiling herself even as she exacts revenge upon him.

In Elizabeth McCracken's mysterious tall tale, "An Early Specimen," set in an idiosyncratic taxidermy and waxworks museum in Florence, a chronically dissatisfied tourist, an American woman, makes a startling discovery—in fact, two discoveries; her story ends as mysteriously as it begins, as we are left with the haunting query the woman has posed to herself—"How would you like to die?" Playful, too, though fueled by a scathing satiric vision, Bernice L. McFadden's "OBF, Inc." portrays a society so thoroughly imbued with racism that an ingenious entrepreneur has commercialized it as public-relations damage control. Here is an insidious political noir in which the targets of racism can profit from it, if they are willing to sell their souls to be identified as the "one black friend" of racist clients: "We live in America, this is a capitalist country, and we monetize everything. *Everything.*" In the third year of the Trump administration, very little in McFadden's American dystopia is far-fetched.

Aimee Bender's lyrically narrated "Firetown" shimmers in a Los Angeles heat wave as a female private investigator becomes involved with a glamorous wealthy client whose husband (and cat) are missing; wife, husband, husband's secretary, and the female "private dick" become caught up in a complicated erotic conflagration, with a wonderfully ambiguous ending.

Similarly, in "Miss Martin," Sheila Kohler's portrayal of a daughter victimized by a charming predator-father is given an inspired turn by the intervention of a unique female presence, a kind of Mary Poppins dispenser of justice—"the perfect secretary, remembers everything, but is utterly discreet, always there when you need her; never there when you don't."

Margaret Atwood, creator of the iconic *The Handmaid's Tale,* as well as more recent environmentally engaged works of fiction (the MaddAddam trilogy, *The Heart Goes Last*), began her career as a poet in the 1960s, in Ontario, Canada; these tersely witty, savagely comic poems are critiques of both patriarchal culture and the strategies of survival by which women accommodate themselves to it in a (seemingly) postfeminist era in which "Everything's suddenly clearer, though also more obscure." In the twenty-first century, women's self-empowerment is in danger of becoming merely gestural, stylized and appropriated without being truly realized, as in fantasies of female autonomy that dissipate in real life when they return to "middle-management black and Jimmy Choos." The poet has no illusions about her role in a world of "moon phases fading to blackout"—"cursed if she smiles or cries." Cassandra Khaw's "Mothers, We Dream" is a captivating tale of seductive sea creatures that claim human husbands, which unfolds like a dream, as in the darkest of fairy tales; only belatedly does the husband think "to ask his wife *what* she was . . ."

Last in the collection, my own story "Assassin" is, like Khaw's, a surrealist excursion into the dark places of the (female) heart. An outspoken woman, a woman no longer concerned in the slightest with presenting herself as attractive to anyone, of any gender, realizes that her redemption will be through an act of assassination, in a cause she perceives to be worthy of self-sacrifice: decapitation of a powerful (male) politician. Taking possession of the severed head, the assassin is (re)possessing her own dignity: "I am thinking, and when I am finished thinking I will know more clearly what to do, and I am not taking bloody orders from you, my man, or from any man ever again."

As in a choral affirmation of female autonomy, female self-identification, and female self-possession, the voices of *Cutting Edge* concur.

Joyce Carol Oates
August 2019

Part I

their bodies, our selves

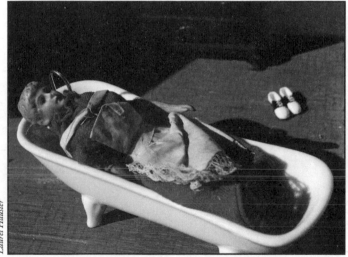

Laurel Hausler

One of These Nights

by Livia Llewellyn

Nicole's father doesn't say a word when he drops us off at Titlow Park, and that's fine with me. Mr. Miller's car is hard and lean and long, with dents all along the side and a giant rusty grille in the front that looks like a monster's grin. His car looks like the kind that would roll down the streets at night all by itself, latching onto you with its lidless glass eyes and running you down like the neighbor's mangy dog, backing up over and over again until there was nothing left but a sticky red smear on the blacktop. His car reminds me of him.

"Time to get wet," Nicole says.

I peel myself off the sticky leather and lurch out of the car and into piercing summer sun and noise, the sounds of a hundred kids shrieking and thrashing in the park's Olympic-sized pool like they're being murdered. From the other side, Nicole unfurls into the humid air, all long, tanned limbs and bikini-top ties, the tips of her black curls wet against her neck from heat and sweat and coconut oil, from secretions of adulthood that still haven't settled over me. I don't understand how she can look so much older, when we're both fifteen. I'm not exactly a kid myself, but the way she's moving forward, I'll never catch up. Then again, I don't have a father like hers to get me there. I have to do everything myself.

"Can I have a dollar for the vending machine, Daddy?" Nicole asks, swaying her body back and forth as if she's still five. She lets the last word drawl and drip out of her mouth, just like I've heard her mother do when she's drunk and itching for a fight.

"Ask your little friend Julie. I already gave her all my spare change."

Nicole's fake smart-ass smile vanishes. Some other type of smile takes its place, and it's real. "I know," she says.

Mr. Miller sneers at her, then flicks his cigarette ash out the window. "You know nothing." Soft gray flecks drift onto Nicole's face.

"You know what's going to happen, don't you."

Mr. Miller shrugs. "Do what you gotta do, Daughter. You know you want to."

"Come on." I tug at Nicole's arm, then touch her tote bag, so heavy it doesn't move. She looks at me, then stares back at him with those same pale green-gray eyes that are in his worn, fox-sharp face. After a second, she slowly walks away. I hook my thumb in the belt loop of my shorts and lean forward slightly, my face hovering just outside the window. He can see right down my top.

I give him my most earnest, respectful gaze. "How about that dollar, Mr. Miller?"

He smiles at me, a wide grin that makes lips curl up like he's pretending he isn't smelling something bad. "Is that all you want from me, honey?" he says, plucking the cigarette out of his mouth. "'Cause Julie asked for more than that, and I gave it to her. I can give you some too."

I lean in closer. "Right here, Mr. Miller? You can't wait?"

"Can you?" He drapes his hand out of the car window, and his thick fingers hang in the air, moving back and forth in front of my breasts as more ash floats from the red tip. A few flecks catch against my skin. He's waiting for me to say it, beckoning it out of me with those rough hands.

A soft pop escapes my lips as they part. But nothing else comes out of me, all my thoughts have gone fuzzy red, and suddenly like thunder the car is rolling across the blacktop, so fast and loud that I jump back in fright. He's gone just like that, out on the road and leaving me behind in a shimmering sea of cars, mothers snarling and tut-tutting at me as they rush their kids past. I don't know why they're glaring at me. I don't control what he does. Most of the time.

I make my way across the lot over to the low building. Paint bubbles and peels off its concrete sides in fading aqua strips, and grime streaks the glass double doors. Above the entrance, fading brass letters read, *TITLOW PARK POOL*, but it's clear that some of the letters have been vandalized and replaced multiple times—*LOW* is spelled with much shinier metal, making the *TIT* that much more noticeable. Like everything in Tacoma, it's seen better times. I like it this way.

Julie Westhoff hangs outside the doors, staring at her reflection in the filthy glass as she sprays something on her long pink tongue. Julie thinks she's more Nicole's friend than I am; even though I knew Nicole first, Julie quickly took her place as the favorite, and treats me as the interloper with the quiet confidence of girls who always look like her. Thin and blond and pretty, always wearing low-cut blouses and halter tops with open spaces that travel down forever. So cool, she's not even a cheerleader, instead standing on the sidelines at pep rallies and games, making all the other girls lose their shit as she leans against the railing and slowly plays with her hair. She's the kind of girl Nicole and I used to wish we could look and act like—above it all, never letting anything get under her skin. It took us awhile to realize there's a world of difference between looking that way and being that way, and we had it going on long before she came around.

"Where's Nicole?" I ask.

"Somewhere, I don't know, she disappeared around the corner. She's pissed at me, or life. I don't know." Julie lets out a small, satisfied sigh as she inspects her face. It always makes her a little satisfied when she thinks we're miserable.

"Is this about her father? Did you two—did you and he . . ." I let my voice trail off.

Julie's eyes narrow. "What the fuck are you talking about? I don't even know him." She looks down at her hand, at the small cylinder rolling between her fingers.

"Really."

"Really." Her voice has turned steely, meaning the conversation is over.

"New poison?" I ask.

Julie points the spray at me. "Open your mouth and find out."

I know my place in the Bermuda Triangle of our relationship. I open my mouth. Julie squeezes the bottle and mists my tongue. A powerful scent of mint hits my nostrils before I taste it, and a small *uck* escapes the back of my throat. Julie started smoking like a chimney when she turned twelve and got boobs, so it's pretty strong. She's probably swallowed her weight in breath freshener by now.

"I thought you didn't like mint."

"Not at first. But the taste goes better with coffee." She

tosses the bottle into her tote bag and gives me a smile and a wink. "And urine. You'll see."

I laugh. "I don't drink urine, you freak."

"If you swim in that pool you do."

"Funny."

We follow a group of parents and their kids through the doors. I can't help but frown at the familiar, nauseating smell of chlorine. We haven't even gotten to the dressing rooms yet and already it clogs my lungs, slowing my movements and weighing me down. It's the smell of my childhood, of graceless flailing, of choking, of always fighting the sensation of sinking into oblivion. Back in '68, the year I turned five, some Tacoma chick won three medals in swimming at the Olympics. By the next summer every mother in the city was dragging her daughter here for lessons, and every summer after that was spent struggling in the lanes of the competition-sized pool, swallowing great gulps of warm chemical water as we thrashed our way through the four-hour sessions like drowning cats. Every summer at least one kid drowned or got sent to the hospital, and they still kept pushing us into the bright blue water, hoping for one more girl who'd bring home the gold. Mom finally stopped taking me when I got my first period and threw a huge shit-fit about wearing a bathing suit with a big old brick of wet cotton between my legs. But I think she was tired of driving all the time, and I was never a good swimmer, anyway. Nicole was the good one. All I learned how to do was hold my breath underwater until the instructors forgot about me or left me alone. It's been a little over three years since I've been here. Nothing's changed.

Well, a few things have. We pay our entrance fees, then make our way into the women's changing room, echoing with high voices and laughter, the slap of bare feet and shower water against tile, the metallic bang of locker doors. It smells the way it always has, like perfume and soap and damp crotch, but the rooms seem smaller and dingier than I remember, and so many girls look younger. As we strip out of our clothes, I catch a girl I recognize from the seventh-grade class staring at me, then some kid on the bench beside her giving me the eye, super young, maybe ten. I realize with a slight start that I've become the unsettling older creature the younger me always wanted to be. The kid's eyes are round and startled as she stares at our naked bodies, at our breasts and the dark hair between our legs. That's how I used to look at the older girls when I was a kid. *Those are women,* I would think to myself. *I'm going to be one of them someday.* And now I am.

"Nicole still isn't here," I say as I set the numbers spinning on the lock. "Did you see her come in?"

Julie makes a sniffing noise. "Maybe she's not coming? I don't really care."

"Did you two have a fight?"

"I'm not fighting with her. She's fighting with me. It's more of a disagreement, really. You know what she's like."

"I don't know, it doesn't sound like her. What is she disagreeing with you about?"

"My rightful place in the world."

I almost laugh out loud—that phrase is so Nicole. "And your rightful place is . . ."

"The one place she can't go."

"There are always places we can't go. Until we do."

"That's not true. You know what I mean. You've seen how she looks at him. She's just jealous of me. Because I can do what she can't."

"I thought you said you didn't know him."

"Well." Julie smiles and rolls her eyes. "Maybe."

"Maybe what?" I stare at her like I don't know what she's talking about, but she only raises her eyebrows and sniffs, gives me that old *you couldn't possibly understand* look, then picks up her towel.

"Ready?" she asks.

"Always."

We make our way through the maze of rooms and into the blinding gold of a late-afternoon sun. It looks exactly the same—the pool seems to stretch on forever, and there's movement everywhere, water and waves and limbs all vibrating and shimmering. *Oscillating*—a word I remember from science class last year. Past the chain-link fence surrounding the pool, the green grass of the park rolls in low waves around a small lake to thick rows of evergreens. Black cables pierce through their branches, converge around high telephone poles, dash across train tracks that line the entire coast. Beyond that, the smooth-pebbled beach and the dark-blue waters of the Sound, which look so warm and inviting and are only ever cold.

"Jesus Christ, this pool is big. Look at all these kids—and their parents, my god. Everyone's so fat and old." Julie's eyes are covered in glasses so dark and large, she looks like an insect. "Why are we here again?"

I shrug. "I met Nicole here—did she tell you? We used to swim here every summer. Four hours a day, five days a week, every June and July for eight years. It's like, this is what summer is to us. It's our ritual."

"Ugh. You are so suburban."

"It wasn't that bad. The lifeguards are handsome—look at *him*."

"I guess. He's kind of . . . What the fuck? How did she get here before we did?"

Julie points to the far opposite corner, to Nicole's slender body wrapped around the base of the lifeguard chair, her wet figure curved against the thick steel poles, her lips moving silently. She's watching the divers at the deep end plunge in, disappearing in one spot and reappearing elsewhere, breaching the surface like miniature whales. The Selkies, that's what they used to call Nicole and me.

"Come on." I lead Julie through clumps of bodies, past the shallow end where groups of parents form protective rings around their toddlers and first-graders, and then down the long side of the pool. I watch the numbers painted on the concrete beneath my feet and just underneath the surface of the water grow larger. It was somewhere past the middle that Nicole and I became comfortable over the years. The shallows are too supervised, and the deep end is for divers, and too empty. The middle is both crowded and deep, but most of all it's deceptive. It's where you can get lost if you become unsure, or if you're overconfident and think you can easily get back to the walls. It's not for amateurs—you have to spend a long time there to learn how to make it all the way back.

"You don't have to swim, you know," I say. "It's fine to just hang out along the side."

Julie's grown a bit more quiet than usual, her fake adult face wrinkling a bit with anxiety or worry, although it's hard to see it under those massive shades. "I know. It's not that I'm against swimming, it's just," she makes a circular motion about her face, "none of this is waterproof. I don't need to look like Alice Cooper, you know?"

"That's fine. We can just hang out by the wall and stare at the guys in Speedos. Like *that* one."

Julie shrugs. "I've seen bigger. I've had bigger. Is Nicole talking to herself? What a psycho."

I shield my eyes and squint. "Oh, that. Yeah, it's nothing. We used to do that all the time here. Just an old habit—going over all the rules and routines we were taught. The way you position your body before you dive, how you move your arms and legs when you do laps, even how and when you breathe. It looks easy, but it's not. It's all very coordinated, like a dance."

I can almost see Julie's eyes rolling underneath her sunglasses. "Wouldn't it be easier to just dance? At least you can drink when you dance . . ." Her voice mutters away into nothingness. For someone who's such a bitch all the time, it's almost sad how the sight of a large body of water is breaking her. I remember all the summers before, all those bullies breaking my nose as they lunged through the water with their raised fists, all the kicks to my sides, all the angry embraces. No one just lets it happen. Everyone fights, to the very end. I have high hopes for Julie. She's a fighter too.

We reach the lifeguard's chair, and now I feel my emotions draining away, and it's the most wonderfully disorienting feeling in the world. It's like everything is underwater now, blurry and distant. Nicole and Julie speak to each other in small sonic waves: they're talking about Nicole's father, and Julie is triumphantly confessing even as Nicole admits tearful jealousy. I meander over to the fence, inspecting the tear in the links that runs up the side of one of the poles. I push the fence, and the tear widens into a body-sized slit: I pull it back, and the fence appears whole again. On the other side, a filthy black garbage bag sags into itself at the pole's base.

I turn back toward the pool. Families are pulling themselves out of the water, lumbering back into the changing rooms as their land-dry replacements make their way toward the shimmering water. It's a pattern, endless and unchanging, but I couldn't tell you what it represents, only that we're not part of it. Julie has taken her sunglasses off and placed them on top of the neat, folded pile of her and Nicole's towels, and she's sitting at the pool's edge, her long legs dangling in the water. Nicole sits next to her, leaning back slightly on one arm that crosses Julie's back. The sun is to our backs, hot and relentless as it slips further down into the day, and goose bumps run up and down my arms, cold bumps that send the fine hairs standing to attention. Nicole motions me over with a tilt of her chin, and I slip next to Julie's free side. We slowly kick our legs back and forth, watching the spectacle of arms and legs and heads rippling before us, fluorescent print-clad bodies on blue foam paddleboards clumsily churning the water. The oily scent of sunscreen wafts through the chlorine-heavy air, clogging my lungs. I stop kicking, and begin to take long, deep breaths as I stare out into the middle of the pool. There's always one place, one perfect place.

Nicole leans farther back, catching my eye. "What's the number?" she asks me.

"58. Same combination as usual."

Nicole shoves Julie's back, sending her into the pool.

I wait for her to emerge, and she does, enraged and flailing. "You fucking bitch, I told you not to do that!" Julie tries to rub her eyes dry, but her wet hands only smear her mascara across her cheeks. With her hair all dark from the water, she really does look like Alice Cooper now. She reaches for the wall, but Nicole slips in, blocking her. I stand up, all of my muscles singing in anticipation.

"You shouldn't have fucked my father," Nicole says, grabbing Julie's slippery arms. "I told you I'd fucking kill you if you touched him." Quick as a flash, she butts Julie's head.

Julie's eyes go wide, and she screams. There's the fight, the anger, along with all the majestic panic that heralds incoming doom: I knew she had it in her. I can't see it, but Julie's kicking out now, trying to push Nicole off her with her feet. We know that trick. We've been in these waters for over a decade.

I watch Nicole kick back and push off from the wall, shoving Julie deeper into the pool's interior. She's laughing, hard and loud, almost screaming like Julie is—it looks like what my mother calls horseplay, or rough-housing. Just two loud girls in a pool filled with a couple hundred other loud girls and boys and men and women all moving like they're having fits. Nicole keeps herding her farther into the pool, pushing her down and pulling her up, getting her good and tired. Julie's choking, she can't fight the water coming into her mouth, she doesn't know the rhythm, the routine. I pace down the side of the pool, never losing sight of them, then back away, take a few quick steps, and I'm in the air. My dive isn't perfect, it's been a year, but I'm powerful and methodical and determined, and I go deep, like I always do. I could always go deepest. Underneath the surface of the water, everything moves about and above me like a tapestry, dappled with blobs of liquid-gold sunlight. I make my way through the floating forest of legs over to Nicole, her bright-cherry ankle bracelet that I wove for her beckoning me near. I pat her right calf twice with the flat of my hand, and then I take hold of Julie's nearest leg, running my hands down until I have her foot. I pull down.

Above me, Nicole is steering us into the most crowded section in the middle. I'm kicked in the head a few times, but that's nothing, there is only the breath that I hold in my lungs, the lean curve of Julie's body rising out of my hand like a dying flower. Nicole pushes her head down one last time, holding it under the water. Julie looks like a mermaid, her hair fanning in waves like silky seagrass. She convulses, contorts, bubbles of air flowing out of her grimacing mouth. Like she's speaking to me, shouting, but no one can hear her down here, below all the muted thunder of the surface. I don't think she even sees me. None of them probably ever have. Her legs stop shaking, and I loosen my grip. Little dots of black start crinkling at the corners of my sight, and my lungs are burning, but I linger for just a second longer, watching how graceful Julie is now, all sleepy-languid and peaceful as she floats. *She's finally dancing*, I think as I shoot past Nicole to the surface, letting the air back into my lungs in one ragged, greedy gasp. I take my time getting back to the wall—Nicole is somewhere in the middle, still holding Julie, maybe telling her some final secret, I don't know. She'll eventually leave her there, wedged between people who don't even understand what's happened, and slip out of the pool and into the changing room, where she'll go to locker 58 and take my tote bag out and get into my clothes and leave. 707 for the combination. It's a lucky number. It hasn't failed us in almost ten years.

I make my way back to the wall and pull myself up. The neat pile of towels is still in place; I'm surprised no one took Julie's sunglasses, so I put them on, and tuck the towels under my arm. I can hear the familiar commotion behind me begin.

No one's going to look at me, I'm completely forgettable. I slip through the long gap in the chain-link fence, and pull Nicole's tote out of the garbage bag. I pull out her dress and sandals and slide them on, then slick my wet hair back from my face with Julie's sunglasses as I serenely walk onto the wide grass lawn. I don't look back. I never look back, it does no good. All across the lawn, families gather up the remains of their picnics, teams pack up volleyball nets, park volunteers shove trash into round cans. Overhead, a sun so dark gold it's almost black drips behind needle-thick trees and into the Puget Sound, and massive bands of orange and purple stain the darkening sky. Afternoon is ending, bleeding out into night. To my left, porch lights begin to flicker like fireflies, and streetlamps glow. I love the sun, but when it starts to die I am most alive.

Behind me, the sirens sing.

Following no particular path, I head toward the intersection next to the train tracks, where several old wooden buildings hunker. Strips of red neon letters flash on and off like a stoplight: *BEACH at TITLOW.* Beneath the tavern sign, several cars are parked, including one that looks like it would slide out from behind bushes in the heat of the night, engine throbbing like the heart of a mechanical minotaur as its fat tires pressed your frozen body against the filthy pavement, grinding you down into motes of blood and bone. This car would follow you to the ends of the earth, its horn crying out to the vast ocean of stars above as it pursued you until you succumbed, until you drowned in the gasoline smoke of its quaking embrace.

This car reminds me of me.

Mr. Miller rolls down the window. "So I guess it's done," he says between long pulls at his bottle of beer. "Another one bites the dust, right?"

I don't say a thing.

He opens the door and stands, stretching. I watch the muscles of his arms stretch and contract under his tanned skin. "She suited the both of you."

"Apparently she suited you too."

"Hey now. Julie was a good girl."

"Uh-huh. Well. I know my rightful place in the world. Julie didn't."

"Well, maybe Nicole can patch things up with her someday. It's not right that you're her only friend."

"I don't know. She took it pretty hard. She was crying when Nicole talked to her. I mean, she was really freaking out—I mean, she acted like she was going to kill herself. Anyway, I don't think she's ever going to speak to Nicole again."

"Damn that girl. She goes through friends like toilet paper."

"Nicole wasn't that bad to her. But you know, she doesn't like competition."

"It wasn't like that. You know it wasn't like that."

"Well, tell that to her the next time it happens."

We lean against the car, watching the distant red and blue lights flash and wink like carnival rides, watching cars whoosh around the wide, clean curve of the park, watching evening slowly creep down into the vast horizon of the Olympic Peninsula. The warm lights of the tavern windows grow brighter, the conversations louder inside, and a cool evening wind spider-steps up my spine and across my neck. We wait until Nicole emerges out of the dark streets, her wet curls pressed flat against her cheeks and forehead, looking as if she's emerging out of some other, faceless girl. She's wearing my clothes. Perhaps that faceless girl is me.

"It's getting late," Mr. Miller says as she walks up to the car. "Time to go home."

Nicole looks amused at his sudden fatherliness. "Since when did you get so concerned about the time? It's not even nine yet."

"Did anyone see you?" I ask.

Nicole bristles. "Did anyone see *you*?" she shoots back.

"What do you think?!" I shouldn't snap at her, she always acts this way after, but I can't help it. It takes a lot out of me too. "You know we have to be prepared."

Mr. Miller sighs, and pitches the empty beer bottle into a nearby trash can, then motions to the car door. "Yeah, this is why we're going home. It's past your dinner and you're getting cranky. Come on now, get in. Backseat, both of you. I've got a case on the front seat."

I slide in after Nicole. She pulls my top off and hands it over. "It's still wet."

"That's fine. Can I give you your dress back tomorrow?"

"Whatever."

"Say, what was going on back there at the pool?" Mr. Miller asks as he heads out of the tavern lot and onto the worn two-lane road, back to our quiet corner of Tacoma, deep in the dry interior of the city, far from ponds and beaches and pools.

"What are you talking about?" Nicole says.

"All those sirens, the ambulances. Someone have an accident?"

"I don't know."

"We weren't there when it happened," I add. "Everything was fine when we left."

"You can read about it tomorrow morning," Nicole says,

as she reaches over to the front seat. "How about one?"

"You know we'll just steal them if you don't," I say.

Mr. Miller laughs. "Just one." He hands Nicole a beer.

I reach across the stiff leather seat, holding out my hand.

Mr. Miller places a bottle into it, but as I draw it toward me, he grabs my wrist. His hand is so large, his skin dark against the white of mine. He lowers his head, and in the dark of the car, I feel his lips against my skin. "Someday, girl," he whispers, his rough whiskers scratching the letters out against my flesh.

He thinks his mouth is a volcano, that my blood is exploding into hot vapor, that my bones are shattering at his touch. He thinks he's going to make me a woman like he did with Julie. That little girl in the changing room knows how a woman is made. He doesn't have a clue. My heart is a cluster of wires, transmitting all the terrible longings from the dark spaces inside my body into Nicole's gelid gaze. We stare at each other, stare at her father, who stares down the black, empty road.

Do we dare? I soundlessly mouth the words to her in the rumbling space of the car.

One of these nights . . . Nicole slides a hand onto my bare thigh, lets it rest there, gentle and warm, so light I can hardly feel it at all.

A History of the World in Five Objects

by S.J. Rozan

She walks into the apartment at 6:32. This is within the window; no adjustments or amends need be made. She removes her pumps and stands them side by side in their space on the closet floor. She places her purse on the shelf by the door and her watch in the bowl beside it. She wears no other jewelry. Two winters ago, on a day of errands, of donning and removing her coat many times, she arrived home to discover she'd lost her mother's gold bracelet.

Baby? Here, baby, I brought you something. Open it, go ahead.

Oh my god, it's so beautiful. Annie, come and look at the beautiful bracelet your daddy gave me.

To make up for last night. I'm so sorry. I'm really sorry. I feel terrible. Does it hurt? You can hardly see it. I'm sorry.

Don't say that. Don't. It doesn't hurt. And it was my fault. You had a hard day. I should have realized.

I just—when you get like that, when you don't listen, when I think maybe you don't love me—

I love you so much!

I just, I can't help myself.

I know. I'm sorry.
Annie, don't touch that. It's not for you.

She undresses, removing piece by piece her Tuesday office ensemble, examining each item. She places the clean and fresh on their hangers and the soiled in the laundry hamper. They will wait there; Tuesday is not laundry day. Nothing requires immediate attention, which pleases her. The soaking and sudsing of clothing is not precisely a disruption. It is necessary often enough that its prospect has been incorporated. Nevertheless, she feels a small exhalation. She buttons her pajama top and walks to the kitchen. She is still getting used to the pajamas. It has only been a month since her mother's nightgown finally disintegrated into its last, unmendable shreds.

God, you look hot in that.
    Honey—
    Take it off. I can't wait.
    Can't we—
    Can't we what? I try to say something nice and you're whining.
    It's just—honey, I hurt all over.
    Oh, for god's sake. Take it off!
    Honey, please. Just tonight.
    What? Are you crazy? I bust my balls all day so you can sit here on your lazy ass and now you give me this shit? Take it off and get over here now. Annie? Jesus, get out of here, Annie. Go!
    Annie, go on. Everything's fine.
    Yeah. Yeah, it's fine. Now take that nightgown off.

Nothing moves in the small apartment but she herself. In retrospect—though she rarely looks back—it might have been better to leave her mother's English ivy with Aunt Lou, who is as good a gardener as her mother was. After that day twelve years ago, when she was released from the hospital—that was only overnight, for observation; she had not been hurt, but she was clearly traumatized, they said, because she'd witnessed the whole thing—and after the police allowed them back in the house, Aunt Lou and Uncle Henry had waited with great patience while she packed some clothes and then wandered through the rooms, choosing what to take with her, now that she was going to go live with them. At that point the English ivy was the only one of her mother's plants left alive. She and Aunt Lou had kept it going over the years. When she moved to her own apartment she brought it with her. Last spring it succumbed to a sudden infestation she didn't know how to fight.

Where are you?

In here.

Oh, for Chrissake. What about dinner?

Ten minutes. It's not quite ready.

It's not? How come you have so much time for these stinking plants but when I come home dinner's not ready? How come?

Honey, it's just another ten minutes.

Honey, it's just another ten minutes. What's wrong with you? You should've been cooking, not screwing around in here. What's this one?

An asparagus fern. No, please don't!

Shit! It scratched me!

Put it back in the pot, please, honey. Please.

Not a chance. No, don't touch it. Go get my dinner. What are you looking at, Annie?

Annie, could you—

No. Leave it, Annie. Leave it there. Nobody clean up this mess until that damn thing is dead, you understand? I want you to watch it die more every day and think about how you killed it. Now go get my dinner.

From the freezer she takes a chicken breast. It's the first from its package of six. Wednesday's six hamburgers sit next to them, and Thursday's lamb chops and Friday's cod. On the other side, Monday's skirt steaks, now down to five. Saturday is eggs and Sunday is cheese and bread, her favorites, but they are high in fat so she limits them. She buys everything in multiples so there is no possibility of running out and having to substitute. It is sometimes necessary to be flexible about vegetables, but she has a mental list of seasonal alternatives—acorn squash when carrots aren't available, for example—and she has never had to go beyond it. With the chicken, as always, it will be rice and peas, on her mother's yellow dish.

God, what is this slop? It's inedible.

It's lasagna. A new recipe. I thought I'd try it.

You shouldn't have. It's terrible.

Maybe try another bite? From the cheese part?

Try another bite? Christ, you sound like my mother! There! Oh, shut up. I don't give a shit who gave you that dish. You put slop like that on it, it deserves to break. Your cousin give you the one Annie has too? Annie, give me yours. Annie hates this shit too, right? Give me that dish, Annie. Give it to me! There, bitch. There!

I'm sorry. I'm sorry. Please.

You'd better be. Now get me a beer and make me a goddamn sandwich. Fast, or the yellow one goes too.

She eats slowly, cutting the chicken breast into precise pieces, setting down her knife and fork between bites. It was quite some time before she was able to touch a knife again, after that day. She finishes, swallows the last of her water, and carries the dish, utensils, and glass to the sink. She pulls on her washing gloves, fills the sink, and soaps the sponge. The sponge is a little stiff, because it's new; she buys a pack of two on the first Monday of each month. Maybe it's that, or maybe she's let her attention wander, just for a moment, or maybe she's grown clumsy; she feels it in slow motion as it happens but can't stop it. The yellow dish slips out of her hand and crashes on the floor.

She stands and stares. That's it, then. She knew this moment would come, and though she did nothing to hasten it, she feels a great relief, an almost giddy buoyancy as a lifetime's weight lifts off her.

She bends and cleans up the mess. Her mother always left everything clean, everything tidy, no matter what messes she and her father made. That day ten years ago was a horror. Blood everywhere. No one to clean it. When she finally reentered the house with Aunt Lou and Uncle Henry, the living room carpet and sofa were gone.

Shut up! Shut up!

   No, honey, oh my god, please stop.

   Shut up!

   Oh god, honey—

   Bitch!

   Please stop. It hurts so much.

   Good! Next time maybe you'll—ow! Ow! Annie? Annie, what the fuck? Put that knife down! I'll—ow! Annie, what are you doing? Are you crazy? Get over here. Oh my god. Annie, you little . . . you . . .

Annie? Oh my god, Annie, what did you do? Annie. You killed him. You killed him! What did you do? Oh, honey! Oh, honey, I'm sorry! Don't die. Please don't. Honey? Get up. I'm sorry. Please get up. Please. Annie. Annie! You killed him. What's wrong with you? Are you crazy? Give me that knife. You—Annie! Oh my god, Annie, stop! Please! Please stop. Ow. Oh. Annie, please.

Once the kitchen is clean and everything is in its place, she removes from the drawer the last of the objects she took with her so long ago. It is not, of course, the same knife with which, according to the police report, her father stabbed her mother before her mother was able to wrest it away and turn it back on him. How terrible it must have been, they all said, for the ten-year-old daughter, whom they found sitting on the living room floor between the bodies. She was covered in blood and staring at her mother's hand, still wrapped around the knife. The police, not wanting to traumatize her further, did not question her. There was no need; what had happened was clear.

She takes the matching knife from the original set of six—she had only brought the one; it was all she was going to need, when the day came—and walks down the short hall to the bathroom. She removes the pajamas and hangs them on the hook. The water comes out cold at first, a quirk of this apartment. She waits until it turns warm and the tub is full. She climbs in with the knife and holds it to her wrist under the water. She is not going to leave a mess.

THE HUNGER

by Lisa Lim

Plumes of cigarette smoke burned her nose hairs as she failed to inhale. Lilly never really learned how to smoke the right way. It was better for her asthma that way. As she ashed on Chin's cold casket she found herself thinking about what fast food she wanted. White Castle or McDonald's? Death always made her hungry.

After a late night of mah-jongg and drinking, Chin stumbled into Mechanics Alley to take a piss and was assaulted by Chinese gangsters. They savagely butchered him and left his dismembered body inside a suitcase in the alley.

Before his demise, Chin drove the Fung Wah bus from Chinatown New York to Chinatown Boston and back. He'd already had a few close calls where he dodged bullets from hooligans of a rival bus company while driving. It was good money, but part of the risk was drive-by shootings.

Chin was found by an old Chinatown local who, while collecting cans in the alley, stumbled upon the suitcase. The old man thought maybe a nice pair of pants would be inside. Instead, he found Chin's blood-soaked clothes, his extremities, and entrails falling out of the suitcase. Including his foot with the bulging bunion that always broke the seams of his shoes.

Chin's mother always duct-taped his shoes so his bunion wouldn't fall out. He was a bona fide mama's boy. Lilly begged Chin for years to get rid of his bunion. But his mother swore it was good luck and a sign of good labor. Lilly hated the way his bunion would rub against her sleeping body. Good riddance to his lucky bunion.

Lilly cursed Chin and blamed his death on spending all his free time drinking too much Johnnie Walker and playing mah-jongg in Chinatown. "Good-for-nothing fried pussy," she whispered in Chinese. He should have been home helping her fold the ten bags of laundered clothes all piled high on their bed. Instead he was about to be buried six feet under in a cushioned casket more comfortable than their bed, resting his tired feet. The bastard.

He had left her with a laundry shop and two girls. Not even boys who could care for her in her old age. Just daughters who she would have to raise alone, and who would abandon her to live with their husbands' families. She always complained about his weak sperm, too weak to give her a boy.

So no. She wasn't about to cry. Tears were for the weak. She had clothes to fold, mouths to feed, and a husband to bury. She didn't have the luxury to mourn. So she smoked. And thought of food instead.

They lived in the back of the laundry shop. Surrounded by clothes and hangers. And since Chin was a hoarder, or as he liked to call it "sentimental," she was left with a hoarder's paradise. Newspapers stacked high enough to reach the ceiling. Old duct-taped shoes piled in boxes like old bones in a cemetery. Ancient radios, some broken, some working, that he and his mother would listen to Chinese opera on. He never liked to throw anything away. No matter how broken.

It was an arranged marriage. So there was no love lost. She wanted so desperately to escape her unhappy childhood home filled with a paranoid schizophrenic mother hurling anxiety, insults, and chopsticks at her in between watching Andre the Giant decimate Hulk Hogan in the ring. Her mother was always rooting for the bully. Her kind. It made Lilly angry that in trying to escape one prison with her raging mother, she had to enter another prison called marriage.

After Chin's death, she looked at a photo of their wedding.
She was so young. Not a line or dark circle to be seen on her
face. But you could still make out a burgeoning sadness in
her eyes. Like weeds, the sadness grew inside her. Without
flinching, she ripped the picture in half, separating her from
her dead husband. They were happier apart.

Her mother-in-law lived with her and her children. It was the Chinese way. You married into a husband's family. That meant letting your in-laws live with you. And suffering every insult and Chinese superstition in stoic silence. Like, "Your mackerel has enough bones to choke all the elderly of Taishan." "What kind of mother lets her children dry wet hair with fans? Fans and AC cause arthritis and asthma." "The gods gave you and your daughters large breasts. Chinese sign of laziness."

Lilly became numb to the insults. Her skin was as tough as beef jerky. Her mother trained her well. Sometimes she fantasized about her mother-in-law's tongue swelling up from anaphylactic shock, causing her to lose her menacing voice. The very thought put a wry smile on her face, and was usually enough to quiet her mind. But this one day was different. As she crouched on the floor, slicing up oxtail for dinner, she heard her mother-in-law utter with disgust, "Such a small tombstone for my son. So damn cheap!"

Suddenly, she felt her blood rushing to her face. Her hands tightening on the neck of the cleaver. It was a reflex. The repeated chopping motion of the cleaver on oxtail suddenly changed direction. It began to swing at her mother-in-law. All her rage for her nasty mother, her weak-spermed husband, her merciless mother-in-law, her lazy, good-for-nothing daughters, the mountain of "sentimental" garbage strewn about the tiny living space, and heaps of unfolded laundry waiting for her. All her rage now swinging. Swinging. Swinging from the cleaver. Until she slaughtered her mother-in-law to bits.

Afterward, she lit a cigarette and felt a strange sudden hunger. And wondered White Castle or McDonald's? Because death always made her hungry.

The End

Too Many Lunatics

by Lucy Taylor

So it's snowing like doomsday, and god only knows where my sister Fiona is—in jail for another DWI or shooting up in a dope house? Passed out in bed with some lowlife or frozen to death in her car?

She doesn't answer her cell—not that I expect her to, but I keep trying. Fiona's thirty-one now, four years younger than me, but she acts like a tantrum-prone ten-year-old. No boundaries and no self-control, just appetite and self-will run riot, as they say in the self-help rooms. Erratic. Last summer, out of the blue, she stopped speaking to me, refused to answer my calls and texted that I'd ruined her life and hell would be too good for me.

Nice.

If trying to rescue my sister means I fucked up her life, then hell yeah, guilty as charged. Sure, I admit I enabled her, which I regret now. I gave her money and paid for her rehab, found her a cashier job at the Kroger I work at, where within two weeks she was caught on tape stealing. Even after that, like an idiot, I gave her a key to my apartment, which she's never bothered to return. Probably tossed it in a dumpster.

Meantime, the snow piles up in drifts while I pace my living room, wondering where she's sleeping and if this frigid winter night will be her last.

When the weather app on my phone flashes a warning that the temp will be zero by midnight—*stay home and get all your pets inside*—I bundle up and head out, then scurry back to retrieve the Smith & Wesson .9mm I keep hidden in the gap between the refrigerator and stove. Maybe silly to take a gun, especially on a night when no one in her right mind would be out, but my first stop will be Quincey's Place, a homeless shelter that sits catty-cornered to Richmond's Monroe Park, where panhandlers prowl and a drug dealer named Ozzie Strand was murdered last summer.

Once on my way, I'm glad I brought a weapon. The way the snow spirals and gusts in every direction makes the night feel chaotic and frenzied, the kind of wild weather that dismantles the natural order of things and brings out the unbalanced and predatory. *Better safe than screwed,* as Daddy used to say when he laid out strict rules for where Fiona and I were allowed to go. *World's full of sickos*, he once said. *Two pretty girls, you're red meat for the psychos and lunatics.*

Did I mention I'm vegetarian?

Still, I figure that was one of the few things Daddy got right. Before a bum liver did him in, he was a claims adjuster for a major insurance company. An obese, boisterous man who appeared to gush confidence, he was hounded by a sense of impending calamity—as though at any moment life would crash down on him like the rotted beams of the condemned buildings he appraised.

He fell apart after Mom left, turned into a barfly with a yen for porn and my sister. Yeah, Fiona. Which I always figured was what drove her to quell her own demons with booze and drugs and back-alley sex.

Quincey's Place is a shoebox-shaped eyesore surrounded

by a ten-foot wrought-iron fence, its finials and spirals now aglitter with ice. The building used to be a warehouse, until a local tobacco magnate bought it and turned it into a homeless shelter in memory of his grandson, who died homeless and strung out on the street. A handful of people huddle outside, grabbing a smoke or walking their dogs, which are kenneled in back of the building. Rules say you have to be clean and sober to get in, but I know Fiona has friends here who'll make sure she gets three hots and a cot no matter what shape she's in.

Inside, a skinny Latino is mopping up puddles of snow-melt on the cement floor while others shove their backpacks and plastic trash bags full of belongings into cubbies along the wall. The smell makes my jaw clench—unwashed flesh and damp dogs and the greasy scent of garlicky stew coming from the dining hall.

The bearded guy at the desk is Cal Smitts, a one-armed Desert Storm vet with a glossy gray ponytail and a belly so massive he could use a wheelbarrow to shove it ahead of him. He hands a locker key to a teenage girl with ebony bangs and a nose ring and says without looking up, "Sorry, Claudia, Fiona ain't here."

I'm surprised he remembers me, but maybe I stand out for some reason. "You got a packed house tonight, Cal. She might've came in and you missed her."

"Nope. Can't get in without goin' past me."

I can see he wants me to move along, but I hold my ground. "Who else is on duty tonight?"

"Just me'n Jesus." He refills a Styrofoam cup from the coffee pot next to him. Makes a point of not offering me any.

"So has she been in lately? When's the last time you saw her?"

"When's the last time *you* seen her?"

"Too long."

"Ever wonder why that might be?"

I ignore his attempt to bait me. "So does she still hang out at J.J.'s? Or has she gotten 86'd from there by now?"

He pulls out a cheap metal coin like the ones Fiona used to collect. "See this? I got twelve years clean and sober, so how the hell would I know who's got kicked out of what bars? Damnit, Claudia, it's snowing like the dickens. Why don't you just run along?"

"And why don't you just—" I stop and remind myself that making a scene won't help Fiona. But I put his name on a mental to-do list.

As I join the crawl of cars up East Broad Street toward J.J.'s, the snow's blowing sideways, blinding me. I take a detour into the sprawling parking lot shared by Big Five Sporting Goods and Piggly Wiggly. Fiona once bragged she had an arrangement with the security guard here—sex in return for not getting hassled about parking overnight. I don't see the guy—lucky for him, because my brakes aren't tip-top and what's to keep me from plowing right into him?

No sign of Fiona's mustard-colored Subaru, but at the Piggly Wiggly loading dock I see a human-shaped bulge under a tarp. As I drive past, a head pops up and shakes off the snow. It's not Fiona, so I go on.

I tried it myself once—you know, sleeping in my car. Just to see what it was like. I took blankets and a thermos of hot tea and parked behind Spoonbread Bistro on West Grace, rolled back the seat, and tried to sleep. By midnight, the cold cleavered through me like I was a side of prime beef. No position was bearable. Nearby glass shattered and footsteps approached. A man puked copiously while two others screamed at each other over who'd stolen a bottle of rotgut. Someone grunted and swore and they zombie-shuffled away, still arguing.

The tea was an error. Soon I found myself crouching behind a hedge, wondering what lurking pervert might be watching while my bashful bladder released only the thinnest streams. I'd forgotten to bring toilet paper. Thighs still wet, I catapulted back into my car and sped home.

I'd lasted less than five hours.

J.J.'s parking lot is almost deserted, but red neon screams *OPEN* from behind dark glass etched with frost flowers and vines. Before going in, I stop at each sedan-shaped mound and clear off enough snow to determine the color. No yellow Subarus, but Fiona might have come here with a friend, so I go in anyway.

"Who?" asks the blond barkeep whose hair looks like it was trimmed with a machete.

I take out my cell and pull up a photo. "Her name's Fiona. Has she been in today?"

Her glance is so brief and dismissive I'm convinced she not only recognizes my sister, but probably knows her all too well. "Dunno. Place has been a zoo all day. Everybody wantin' to get a buzz on before Snowmageddon."

"She drinks Stoli with cocktail onions, if somebody's buying. Beer if they're not. Used to hang with a guy named Ozzie Strand, but he died."

"Condolences," she smirks, rolling her eyes as she leans tatted-up arms on the bartop. "Look, hon, you wanna drink, I can serve you. Information, not so much. What'll it be?"

"Diet Coke," I say, heading over to check out the john.

Only one woman's in there and she's shooting up in a stall.

I throw down a few ones and get out.

A gangly guy with eyebrows thick as matching mustaches intercepts me just inside the door. He reeks of gin and desperation and keeps glancing over his shoulder like he's scared the bartender will see him chatting me up.

"Heard you say you're Fiona's sister?"

Did I? I can't remember.

He leans close, exhaling alcohol fumes in my face while scratching the side of a nose speckled with blackheads. "Yeah, I see her in you. The green eyes. Tortoiseshell eyes."

"We're just half sisters," I blurt out for no reason. Maybe I'm trying to make it clear that Fiona and I are very different and that our connection is more tenuous than full sibling-hood, but instantly I'm annoyed at myself for lying. What do I care what this lush thinks of me?

"Fiona and I go way back," he confides, "but she ain't got time for me now. Only parties with her new besties."

"Yeah? And they are . . . ?"

He props his chin with a hand, mimes deep thought. "Well now, my brain's fogged. Might need another shot or three to boost my recollection."

I pull out a twenty, then another when he scorns the first offer. Feigning reluctance, he recites an address in the Fan District. "Travis and Mona's place."

"Is Fiona there now?"

"Can't say. Could be. She hangs with 'em sometimes. Travis, he's a movie buff, you get my drift." In case I don't, he hinges at the waist and bares a sad conglomeration of dis-colored teeth. "Fiona, she likes to get high and eat pussy. Travis likes to watch. Invites his buddies over to enjoy the show and partake. How 'bout you? You like to eat pussy?"

He snakes a hand toward my crotch. I jump back, hands balled into fists, but in the thick gloves I'm wearing, how much harm can I do? Still, something in my stance or expression frightens him, because he backs away and calls out as I leave, "Hey, I take it back. No way are you like Fiona. She's *hot!*"

The address on Floyd Avenue isn't far, but in the whiteout I take a wrong turn and wind up on Monument Avenue at the statue of Jeb Stewart, blanketed in white like an equestrian wraith. I'm driving too fast. When I hit ice, I forget everything I know about winter driving and slam the brakes. The car careens into the oncoming lane. I overcorrect, bounce off the curb, and shatter the headlight of a parked SUV. The energy of the collision bangs through my unbelted body and slams my forehead into the dash.

Stars flare and black bars frame my vision. I'm drifting between two places and times, unsure which is real, my memories strewn haphazardly like odds and ends from a pilfered purse. My stomach heaves and there's a fruity-sick burn in my gorge—Daddy's Beam swigged on the sly. The head-jarring whomp the whiskey delivers releases a surge of rage and bravado. A choice must be made—what will it be?—and when that fifteen-year-old girl I used to be looks down at her hands, she's more thrilled than shocked to see her choice is the claw hammer.

Guns abound in this house, of course, for hunting and defense, and the kitchen offers a seductive array of knives. But the claw hammer has its own allure—it's brutally, unequivocally *male*. As I heft it, I wonder if this is what men feel when they get a hard-on, when they swagger into a bedroom to *fuck*.

In Daddy's room, I stand above him and wonder if this primitive power is what he feels as he enters my sister's room—enters my sister. Spent now, he snores and snorts, a bull pawing the sod in his sleep. I raise the hammer—where to start, the crease between the heavy brows or the crooked bridge of the nose, the fleshy, flapping lips that frame a cavernous mouth?

Then a presence heretofore unnoticed or ignored soundlessly usurps my mind, and it commands all my attention. It's me and not me, this voice of sanity and reason. It reminds me of the price I'll pay: a lifetime caged in prison or a mental ward, *the girl who killed her daddy,* all freedom lost, hope gone.

I leave my father's room and never venture there again. No one but me ever knows what I almost did.

Violent shivering shakes me awake. The headlights illuminate an SUV impaled upon my bumper, but the street is silent, eerily pristine. No one's come outside to confront me, and I take this as an omen. Uncoupling the two vehicles with as little scrape and complaint of metal as possible, I soldier on.

Travis and Mona share a row house with a handsome pedimented porch and snow frosting the spindlework and eaves. I pound the knocker until a blurry figure ghosts behind the beveled glass and a male voice snarls, "Whozit?"

"I'm Fiona's sister. I'm here to take her home."

A long pause, then: "She's left."

"Where'd she go?"

"Don't know."

"I was told she's here."

"You were misinformed."

He's lying, I'm sure of it. Fiona may be passed out drunk or OD'd. She may be held against her will.

"Look, I need to talk to you. I don't want to call the cops to do a wellness check on her, but if you don't let me in—"

He curses colorfully and loudly before opening the door, a short, paunchy man too puny for his sportscaster's voice who glares at the windblown snow as though personally offended. "Fuck, this shit's still coming down." Turns his bleary gaze on me. "So you're Claudia?"

He knows my name. That's good. It means Fiona's spoken of me.

"I need to see my sister. She's not answering her phone."

"And I told you she's not here." He gazes into the white, swirling sky, tugs at the waistband of his baggy sweats. "Damn this snow."

"Travis, let me come in. I'm freezing out here."

"What the fuck, she told you my name? Big mouth she's got, your sister. Course, that's sometimes to my advantage."

With the creep gloating over Fiona's oral talents, I try to dart into the house, but he plants a palm on my chest and shoves me back. Slams the door so hard that snow showers down from the frame.

This time when I bang on the door, he ignores me.

The wind bullies and whips me as I stumble back to the car. It's only because I'm using the parked vehicles for balance that my hand brushes a cascade of snow off a fender, revealing the distinctive mustard-colored paint job. I check the license plate. It's hers.

My hunch was right. She's in there.

This time, rather than knock, I try the knob. The door

opens, but before I can get ten feet into the house, Travis comes charging up the hall, red-faced, flailing his arms. "Who said you could come in here? Get the hell out!"

"Fiona's car's outside! She's here!"

"So what? She had someplace to go. Her piece-of-shit car wouldn't start, so I let her take my wife's."

"I don't believe you. Where would she go in a snow-storm?"

"Why is it any of your damn business?"

"It's my business because you feed her drugs and pass her around for your friends to fuck and because she's too sick to understand you're using her!"

Except for a twitch in his upper lip, he's very still, but when he speaks, his voice is infused with a new level of malice. "Fiona told us all about you. She warned us you're dangerous. She hates you and never wants to see you again. Why don't you leave her alone?"

I'm as stunned as if he'd bludgeoned me with a brick, but I know he's lying, and that gives me courage. I yell Fiona's name and bolt for the stairs with him right behind me. Half-way up, he grabs me and spins me around, which compounds the force when he hooks a fist into my jaw.

My head snaps to the side. My knees liquefy and I plop down on the stairs. He looms over me, fist drawn back to punch me again, so I pull out the .9mm and fire a shot at his face.

The world implodes. He bares his teeth, and his eyes blaze black murder as he lunges for my throat. In despair and disbelief, I realize I've done the impossible—missed a target three feet away.

Then his mouth jerks askew, and he folds up like laundry—

knees, waist, and neck—before doing a face-plant on the step below me. A tooth flies from his mouth and lands in my lap. Blood burps from the hole in his back.

Above me, a woman screams like the love of her life has just died. I look up to see a woman I presume to be Mona, coal-eyed and keening, clutching the bannister and flopping down the steps in a bra-and-panty set that's seen better days. This time, I aim. One side of her face shears off from her skull and she crashes past, landing with her thighs spread over her man's head in a tragic parody of cunnilingus.

I find myself wondering if she'd have worn better undies had she known she was going to die in them today.

Stepping carefully around the blood, I race upstairs to find Fiona.

My worst fears are confirmed.

She's not there.

The journey home is a careening, sliding, stop-and-skid ordeal. Streetlights blink mindlessly. Ditched cars block intersections, their feckless drivers gone. I drive over curbs and plow across lawns.

When I finally make it home, I'm horrified to discover my living room is a shambles. I've been burglarized, and to judge from the noises coming from the back of the house, it's still going on. In the kitchen I surprise a trench-coated figure in a black woolen cap with one shoulder planted against the refrigerator, trying to muscle it away from the wall.

In the most commanding voice I can muster, I yell, "Hold it right there!"

The intruder whirls. "Shit, you're home!"

"Fiona?"

She yanks off the cap. Bleached hair with brown roots tumbles around her thin face. Her blue eyes dart wildly. She looks cornered and feral.

"What the hell are you doing?"

She whips out a key on the end of a plastic fob and waves it in front of me like a priest warding off evil with a minuscule cross. "You gave me this, remember? You said to stop by anytime."

"I didn't say to ransack my house!"

Rather than explain or apologize, she goes on the attack: "What are you doing back so soon? Cal called me from Quincey's and said you were there looking for me, that you were making the rounds. I thought the snowstorm would slow you down."

"Why would Cal—" But I know, of course, and the weight of that feels like an avalanche crashing onto my shoulders. "You told him to call if I showed up, didn't you? Why would you do that, Fiona? Is it because you hate me and never want to see me again?"

She bounces on her feet, all manic energy. "That's a weird question."

"Travis told me that's what you said. Is it true?"

"It's—wait, what? How do you know Travis? Have you been following me? Christ, tell me you didn't just show up at his door, 'cause if you did, you've got me in a world of hurt. Somebody violates Travis's privacy, he can get mean."

"Oh, I think I violated more than his privacy."

"You were at his house? Shit, now he's gonna think I gave you his address. What did you say to him? Did Mona see you? Fuck, I'd rather have Travis pissed off at me than *her.*"

"Yeah, Mona saw me. We didn't talk, though."

"Thank god for that at least. Damnit, Claudia, you've got no right harassing my friends."

I look at the mess she's made—drawers emptied out, oven door open, broken crockery. "Fiona, what were you looking for here? What did you think you'd find behind the refrigerator?"

I already know the answer, of course, but it's amusing to watch her mentally trying out lies before, defeated, falling back on the truth. "Look, I know you have a gun. I figured you'd hide it someplace obvious like in the bookcase or the closet. Then I remembered how Daddy used to always stash a bottle or two behind the refrigerator at home until you got wise to him and threw them out. So it came to me, hey, I bet that's where you'd hide your gun. I was wrong. You're not that stupid. You probably pitched it in the James River. Hell, that's what I woulda done."

It takes me a moment to get my breath back so I can speak. "Why would I do that, Fiona? I don't understand."

Whether it's exhaustion or pharmaceutical disinhibition, she rattles on, "You'd've had to get rid of the murder weapon, wouldn't you—after you killed Ozzie. You followed him into the park that night and you shot him. I can't prove it yet, but I know you did. Travis has some experience with this kind of stuff. He told me if I could find the gun, the cops could match it to the bullets that came out of Ozzie."

"What do you care who killed Ozzie? He beat you. He was a violent, abusive scumbag."

"He loved me."

"He deserved whatever he got. Just another piece of shit. Like Travis. Like Daddy."

She gapes at me like I just spit on God.

"What, you thought I didn't know why he went to your room all those nights, what he was doing?"

She starts to cry—big, ugly sobs. It's a disgusting performance, but when she's finally able to talk, I hear her out.

"It wasn't like that! For fuck's sake, he was reading me bedtime stories at night, because you were too old for them and because he knew I had bad dreams. And sometimes he cried too, and I comforted him, because he knew he was an alcoholic, but he couldn't stop, and he hated himself for it. But he never touched me the way you think. You're wrong about that, just like you were wrong about Ozzie!"

Even now, after all this time, Fiona's capacity for denial, her ability to rescript history, never ceases to stun me.

"The only thing I ever wanted was to protect you and keep you safe. Why is it so hard for you to believe that?"

So I tell her about the one thing I swore I'd never tell anyone: that night when I snuck into Daddy's room and raised the hammer over his head, trying to decide what part of his face I would smash first. I tell her how the voice in my head stopped me from going through with it. "You're the only person I've ever told."

When I finish, she isn't crying. Her eyes look like chips of blue ice, colder than anything I've seen in my life that was still drawing breath.

"I'll tell you a secret too, Claudia. Ozzie drove for Travis and sold product out in Henrico and King William County. He was important to Travis's business. Him dying was a gut punch to Travis. Finding who killed him was important too." She pulls out her phone.

"Fiona, don't. We can talk about this. Don't call the cops."

"Who said anything about the fucking cops?" She turns

away and starts speaking into her phone. "Hey, Travis, it's me. Coupla things. First off, I apologize about my sister coming to your house. I had no idea, swear to god. Second, I was right. She as good as confessed. You know where she's at, so when you get this, do what you have to. She killed Ozzie. I don't give a shit what happens to her anymore."

She ends the call. Looks surprised but not especially alarmed when she sees I'm pointing the gun at her. "Shit, you had it on you the whole time. I shoulda known."

I don't say anything, because I know silence frightens her.

Pretty soon she starts getting antsy and has to talk: "Oh come on, Claudia, put that away. I was just trying to pay you back for what you said about Daddy. That wasn't Travis I called. I was just pretending . . . Claudia? C'mon, Claudia, talk to me."

She doesn't understand that I'm waiting for the voice of sanity and reason to stop me before I pull the trigger. But it hasn't got a goddamned thing to say.

Please Translate

by Edwidge Danticat

[Translator's Note: We were asked to translate from Haitian Creole to English the following phone messages from Sauvanne Philippe Guillaume to her estranged husband Jonas Guillaume, father of five-year-old Jimmy Guillaume. We are professional translators certified by the city of Miami and state of Florida, license number CT09956 on file, if requested.]

Message #1: Hi. Just calling to see how you two are doing. I'll call later. All right? All right then.

Message #2: Hi. Wow. Please call me back.

Message #3: Jonas, I wish you would call me back. I'm waiting for him. I have work tomorrow. I picked up an extra Saturday shift. Mama's going to watch Jimmy for me after you bring him home.

Message #4: Jonas, I just want to hear from you. I hope everything's okay.

Message #5: Jonas, is everything all right?

Message #6: Jonas, where are you?

Message #7: Jonas, it's almost midnight. Where are you?

Message #8: Jonas, I'm coming over there to get my car. [*Muttering.*] Why did I let that thief borrow my car. [*Louder*] Jonas, I only let you borrow my car so Jimmy could be safe in a proper car. Your car wasn't in the shop, was it? I can't believe I was fooled by you again.

Message #9: Okay, Jonas, I'm very worried now. I'm going to call someone to bring me over there.

Message #10: Goddamnit, Jonas, it shouldn't take this long to get some ice cream. Where are you with my son? In the middle of the night.

Message #11: Jonas! Jonas! I want my child.

Message #12: Jonas [*sobbing*], Jonas, please. Where have you taken my child?

Message #13: [*Inaudible.*]

Message #14: [*Screaming*] JONAS!

Message #15: [*Calmer*] Jonas, please bring my baby back. I promise I won't leave you. I'll stay with you. We can go to Pastor David and get some counseling, for Jimmy's sake. Please, Jonas, just please answer this phone.

Message #16: You're not a policeman here, Jonas. You have

to follow the law here. Just like everybody else. Jonas, here you're just like everybody else.

Message #17: I wanted to avoid this, Jonas, but this is your last chance before I call the police. You better call me, you illegal mother— Okay. Please, Jonas, please let me know my baby's okay.

Message #18: Jonas, listen to me. I'll take this as far as you want me to. If you think you have more balls than every other man in the world, I'll show you you're wrong.

Message #19: Jonas, I love you. I really do. Just please bring my baby back now. Please.

Message #20: Jonas, is this about the car? I told you I paid for it myself. Marcus did not help me. You're jealous for nothing, Jonas. He's my boss, that's all, my supervisor. Yes, he promoted me at the hotel, but that had nothing to do with me and him being together. I mean we're not together, Marcus and me. I'm not together with him. And I'm not together with you. Please just bring my baby back.

Message #21: Jonas, you were my first love. Ever since we were kids in Haiti. I have always loved you. I'm not going to stop loving you for someone I've just met. I would never demean you like that, Jonas. Please believe that.

Message #22: My baby Jonas. Please. [*Muttering.*] I should have never trusted that good-for-nothing.

Message #23: You're still sour about Marcus buying me that car, huh, Jonas? You're holding my child hostage over a man and a car. Then you know what? You're no man at all. The police are coming now to your place. The real police of this country. And I'm coming with them.

Message #24: Jonas, everyone knows I'm the one who bought that car. Marcus just gave me a ride to the dealership. He helped me bargain down the price. I bought it all by myself.

Message #25: Jonas, I'm never going to let you do this to me again. I'm never going to let you take my child again and just turn off your phone and scare me like this. It's the last time. I'm telling you. The last time.

Message #26: Jonas, this time I'm really going to call the police. You think I'm afraid to because I don't have my papers. Are you hoping they'll deport me so you can keep my son? Marcus is a better man than you, Jonas. He gave me that job even without my papers. Screw the papers, Jonas. Even if I get deported back to Haiti, I'm taking Jimmy with me. Screw everything, Jonas. Next time you hear from me, you'll hear sirens too. I'm going to be in a police car and I'll be on my way to your house, Jonas. You better believe that.

Message #27: Don't push me, Jonas. You know I can do it and I will. You better just bring me back my child. I'm going to call Marcus too. He'll give me a ride and the police will get my baby from you. They'll arrest you and deport you, but not before I give Marcus a big kiss right there in front of your ugly face.

Message #28: Jonas, please. I'm sorry. I'm sorry. I just said all that to make you angry. I'm sorry, baby. I'm sorry, darling. Please forgive me. Please, please forgive me.

Message #29: Jonas, I'm still giving you a break. I lied. I haven't called the police on you yet, but if you push me I will. It's now two a.m. [*Inaudible.*] I am going to give you fifteen more minutes to bring my child and my car back. See, I'm still trying to make things easier for you, Jonas. Please bring our baby back. Please. Please bring him back.

Message #30: Jonas, can you hear the phone ring? Are you looking at my number and not picking up? Did you fall asleep? Is Jimmy asleep?

Message #31: Jonas, I'm calling the police now for real, Jonas, and I'm going to take a taxi all the way out there. I'm going to come and get my baby from you. Even if it costs a hundred dollars I don't have. I'm going to come all the way out to Miramar where I think you are, you stupid liar and kidnapper.

Message #32: Okay, Jonas, I realize that if it's your child, you can't kidnap him. I know. I'm sorry for accusing you. I know you would not kidnap our child just to punish me. Please just bring him back. I am sorry for everything I've said. Please forget everything I've said.

Message #33: Jonas, you're proving yourself to be a very low-class individual. If you think you're going to fuck with me, I'll show you. You're messing with me for the last time. You jealous piece of shit.

Message #34: [*Inaudible.*]

Message #35: [*Inaudible.*]

Message #36: [*Sirens blaring, mostly inaudible. Sobs.*]

Message #37: Jonas, how can you do this to our baby? [*Man's voice follows:*] YOU WORTHLESS MOTHERFUCKER, YOU ARE GOING TO DIE!

Message #38: [*Loud background voices. Sobs.*] Jonas, you should not have run and left Jimmy behind like that. Jonas, you should have killed yourself too.

Message #39: Jonas. [*Woman screaming:*] I WILL FIND YOU! WHEREVER YOU ARE, I WILL FIND YOU!

Message #40: Jonas, I will spend the rest of my life looking for you. [*Screaming. Sobs.*] Oh my god, Marcus. I can't believe he did this to my baby.

Message #41: Jonas, you stupid asshole. I can't believe you did this to our child. I knew this phone would lead them to you. It's like having a GPS on you, you imbecile. You can barricade yourself in there all you want, but they're going to get you. And if you try to run they're going to blow you right out of this world. No court sentence will be enough for you, though. Even if you make it out alive and go to jail. One day I will kill you with my bare hands. I will put your face in water and drown you the same way, just like I have now a thousand

times in my mind. I'm going to show you, Jonas. I'm going to—
Recorded Message: *This customer's mailbox is full.*

[End of translation.]

Part II

a doom of one's own

The Boy without a Bike

by Jennifer Morales

Beni's trailer park clings to a hill that juts out of a cornfield, smack in the middle of nowhere. Wild things run through all the time—coyotes, foxes, deer, snakes, turkeys, skunks, not to mention the rabbits and squirrels I see all the time in Milwaukee.

I'm not afraid of the animals, but sometimes the people freak me out.

Beni moved out to the country a year ago to get her son, Adán, away from bad influences in the city, but I can't say that where she landed is much better. Take the situation with Adán's bike, for instance. Somebody stole it.

That's why I'm out here tonight, crawling along the dark country roads looking for the turn into God's Country Mobile Estate. Beni says she wants me there to help her figure out who took the bike, but I think what she really wants is for me to buy Adán a new one. Like I'm made of money.

And I miss you, she'd texted. *Come on come spend the weekend out here I'll make it fun.*

I thought I was done trying to make Beni happy, but here I am, rolling up to her trailer, ready to do whatever she asks.

Maybe I'm lonely. It's been a busy year since we broke up. I finished my carpentry apprenticeship and got a construction job, which hasn't left me with much time or energy for making new friends or even seeing the ones I already got.

Maybe it's Adán. Beni's kid was pretty much my kid too, for the couple of years she and I were together. I miss him, his acorn head with the eyes too big for his face, the crap he was always pulling, like using the blank pages of my apprenticeship notebooks to draw his horses. So many horses, page after page. Annoying as hell when we lived together, but somehow—with the distance of a year and a couple hundred miles—it almost seems cute.

The road winds past the first set of trailers, a V-shaped cluster of eight in various stages of decay, then up a hill. At the top, the road splits into two around the landlords' trailer where, in the flash of my headlights, someone moves a curtain in the kitchen to peer out. I wave, unsure if the person can see me. The two branches of the road take you to an upper tier and a lower, each with about six or eight more trailers. Beni lives on the lower tier.

I pull into the short gravel drive and study her place before turning off the headlights. It's getting on the end of October and Beni has Halloween paper cutouts up across the front windows. A few Día de los Muertos calaveras are in the mix, papel picado of lacy Mexican skulls crowded by drugstore spiders and a jack-o'-lantern, a Dracula figure lurking over it all.

I get my duffel bag from the backseat and straighten up to listen to the night. Late-season crickets, some coyotes in the distance, the static-boom-gunfire rush of the next-door neighbor's video game. Beni's strict voice calling to Adán from inside.

I feel the outside pocket of the duffel. The ziplock is still there. Sell that, and Adán's got a new bike plus something left over for me to enjoy. Maybe a treat for Beni too.

"You came," Beni says upon opening the door, but she doesn't appear all that surprised.

"Hey." I lean in to give her a kiss on the cheek. She looks good, her dark hair swept back into a ponytail, her skin glowing. "Country air's been good for you."

"Thanks."

"Smells good in here."

"Mole rojo. There'll be chicken enchiladas in about half an hour."

"Excellent." I'm not sure I miss being in a relationship with Beni, but memories of her cooking do keep me up at night once in a while.

Adán comes into the kitchen. He's getting plump, a little soft in the hips.

"Paula!"

He's too big for it but I let him jump into my arms.

"What? I don't see you for a few months and you go and grow three feet on me?"

He blushes. "Just a couple inches. Mom's mad she had to buy me all new pants for school."

"I bet she is." I set him down with a grunt.

"You want to go look for bats?" Adán asks.

"No bats. Let Paula rest for a minute, will you?" Beni waves a spoon at him. "You go back and finish your homework. Then you'll have the whole weekend free to bother Paula."

Adán groans, his shoulders slumping like wet clay, but he does as he's told. When he's back in his room, he cranks up the radio until the wall shakes.

"You have a little teenager on your hands." I tilt my head toward the reverberating wall.

"Yeah. But he's still a good kid."

"Yeah." I watch Beni move around the kitchen, washing a few dishes and wiping down the counter. Her tight jeans show off her curves and I remember the evening we met, salsa night at a lakefront gay bar in Milwaukee.

"You want a beer?" she asks.

"That would be great."

She gets me a Corona from the fridge and pours it into a glass. As she sets it in front of me on the kitchen table, she taps my shoulder where the duffel bag still hangs.

"You can put that down, you know. Stay a while."

"Right." I let the bag slide to my feet and kick it under the table.

Beni is standing close, her brown eyes playful. "Got something in there to share with me later?"

"Yeah, but not what you're thinking, Beni." I take a drink of the beer.

"No?" Now she's holding onto the edge of my shirt and giving it a tug.

"No, Beni—I'm not here to—" I take a step back and pull out a chair and sit in it. "I don't think we should sleep together."

"Suit yourself." She goes to the fridge and gets herself a beer, sits across from me. She's gnawing on the inside of her lip, the way she does when I disappoint her.

I half knew she wanted more than help with the bike when she texted, but I showed up anyway. Beni's a beautiful woman yet our life together was more complicated than I like. She was always trying to be both my girlfriend and my mother—and I definitely don't need another mother. And then there's Adán. Love that kid, but I'm not sure I have what it takes to be his parent.

I try to change the subject: "Adán's bike? You think it got stolen?"

"I know it got stolen."

"How do you know?"

She pops her beer can open with a knock and a hiss. "Because it's gone."

"Maybe he left it somewhere."

"No, not that bike. You know how much he loves it."

I do know. Six months ago, my wallet fat with my first real carpenter paycheck, I took Adán to the bike store and let him pick out the one he wanted. I hardly even winced when the sales guy turned over the price tag: three hundred bucks.

"And it's somebody here in the trailer park that took it." She sets her beer down hard on the table, like she's making a point in an argument I didn't even know we were having.

"What makes you say that?"

"Because look where we are, Paula. Six miles from town, hidden away in the woods on a winding road. Even people who have lived in this area their entire lives don't know we're up here."

"And your landlords watch this place like hawks." I remember the figure at the window when I drove in, the curtain twitching open then closed. "Okay. Who do you think took it?"

"I don't know. A kid, probably. Or maybe someone stealing shit and selling it for drug money."

"Hard drugs, you mean." I think of the weed in the bag at my feet.

"How would I know what kind of drugs?"

"Um, speaking of which, after dinner I have to run a little errand. Does that guy Dean still live out here, in the blue trailer?"

"Yeah." Beni makes a noise like she's going to spit. "Dean."

"What's that about, that face?"

"That guy is a slimeball. I've lived out here for a year and I swear I can't walk out to the damn mailbox without him hitting on me twice. Once on the way there and once on the way back."

"Doesn't he know you're gay?"

Beni huffs. "Oh, you know the type. The kind that thinks he can turn you straight with the love of the right man." She leans back in her chair and grabs her crotch like she's got something in her pants.

"I hate those guys," I say, but I don't want to dwell on his pants. I'm more interested in what he's got in his pockets. "You think he's interested in making a little purchase?"

"Oh, that's what's in the bag." Beni gives me a look. "I thought you came out here to see me and Adán, and help with the bike situation."

"That's what this is about. The bike situation. In case we don't find it. I need some cash to get him a new one."

"I thought you were done with that stuff, now that you have this good-paying job."

"I am, mostly. It's just, this is important and I don't have anything saved up yet. It takes awhile to get back on your feet."

"Tell me about it." She waves her hands at me from across the table. "I never liked it, you dealing." There's a hardness in her eyes, but a sadness too.

We're caught in that semi-recent-lesbian-breakup phase where we still have the right to worry about each other and tell each other off, but not the right to do anything about it. I'm relieved when her tone shifts toward self-interest.

"You know, I don't want to get a reputation out here for being the drug house," she says. "You're going to get me kicked out."

"It's not a drug house if the drugs aren't *in* the house. And anyway, this is the last time it's going to happen. I'm going to buy that kid the toughest bike lock in the store. And if he doesn't lock the bike up, I'm going to come back out here and give him the chanclazo of his sorry little lifetime. *Kpow!*" I act out swatting Adán's behind with a house shoe and Beni can't help but laugh.

She gets up from the table and says, "Okay, fine. Run your little errand after we eat. Just don't let Adán know where the money's coming from, okay? And don't let the neighbors know either."

"Not a word."

After dinner, Adán and I go out to the tiny front yard to watch the bats swoop in and out under the streetlight.

"Did you know that a single bat can eat six thousand insects in one night?" Adán says. "But this year a lot of them got sick and died from nose fungus, so there's more bugs."

"Nose fungus, huh?" I look at his upturned face, a mix of adult seriousness and eight-year-old goofy self-satisfaction. "Where'd you learn all that?"

He shrugs. "I like to read about animals. We had to do an animal report in science and I chose the brown bat. And sometimes I go over to Badger's house and we watch Animal Planet before his dad gets home. He's got cable."

"Badger? A friend from school?"

"Yeah. And he lives here. His real name is Robert or something but his dad calls him Badger."

"Because he likes sports? Like the Wisconsin Badgers?"

"No! He's like me."

"What do you mean?"

Adán turns his attention from the bats overhead to his feet. "I don't know. He just doesn't like sports."

"But he likes animals as much as you do?"

Adán nods and I reach out to rub his head.

"That's good, kid. It's good you've got a friend."

Beni calls him in and I follow, to say goodnight and retrieve the ziplock. I text the number I have for Dean from the last time, three months ago.

Come on over, he replies. *U remember which trailer?*

In most businesses, they talk about the middleman. In this transaction, I am like the middle-middle-middleman. Somebody brought the stuff to Milwaukee in a big shipment, like a U-Haul full, from Mexico or California—farm fresh. Then a bunch of guys in Milwaukee divvied it up to sell to people like me. And then here I am, hoping to get Dean to bite on a half-gallon bag to supply the neighborhood.

"Oh, wow," Dean says, leaning back into his filthy couch. "That's good shit."

"Right?"

He passes me the joint but I don't take more than one hit. I can't get foggy on the job.

"Yeah." He's lost for a second, his eyes drifting to the television where a fishing show is playing on mute. Then he's back to business. "I'll take it. That is one product I can definitely endorse. Can't get shit around here that's worth pissing on, let alone smoking."

"So you'll take the whole bag?"

Dean doesn't seem to hear me. "Speaking of pissing on things, I'll be right back."

He ambles off to the bathroom. Not ten seconds later I sense a presence in the dim room.

"Dad?" It's a child's voice, a boy.

"Hey, little man. Your dad's in the bathroom. I'm Paula."

The boy emerges from the darkness that crowds either side of the wide TV screen. "Who are you?"

"Paula, I just said."

"Yeah, but I mean . . ." He rubs his eyes. "Are you Dad's girlfriend?"

I laugh. "No, not by a long shot. I'm Paula." I reach out my hand for him to shake and he takes it in his for a split second. "I'm a friend of—do you know Adán, here in the trailer park? You two seem about the same age."

Now the child's face grows bright. "Yeah. He's my friend. We're in the same class."

"Wait. You're not Badger, are you?"

He nods.

"Adán was just telling me about you."

"He was?" I can see all of Badger's teeth glinting in the TV light. They're too big for his third-grader mouth.

"Yeah, about watching Animal Planet and not liking sports."

"Who doesn't like sports?" Dean walks back into the living room, tightening his belt. He reaches for Badger's shoulder. "This kid loves football. And hockey. Don't you?"

Badger gives half a nod before Dean says, "Go back to

bed. Paula and I have some grown-up business to take care of here." He winks at me in a way that turns my stomach.

"Hey, Badger, before you go, can I ask you a question?"

"Sure, I guess."

"Do you happen to know what happened to Adán's new bike?"

This kid is as blond as they come, with the pale skin that goes with it. So pale that even in the TV light I can see he's flushed pink, pajama collar to hairline. He may not be the thief, but he knows something.

"Not a chance. Badger doesn't have anything to do with that little faggot." Dean turns to his son and laughs. "Do you, boy?"

Badger's body is taut. He seems ready to spring, alive inside like an animal being watched, though he doesn't speak. When his father excuses him to go back to bed, it's almost as if he melts, disappearing into the trailer's frog-green carpet.

Dean returns to the couch and sits too close to me. The chunky Zippo lighter he used to light the joint is pressing into my thigh through the pocket of his jeans.

"So, you doing anything after this?" he asks, his eyes carving into the V-neck of my shirt. "Or anyone?" He smiles at his own joke. It's an imprecise, sloppy smile—the weed has him floating—but somehow he can manage to slip a hand between my legs, right on target.

I jump up and yell, "You know I'm gay, right?"

That snaps him out of it and he draws back like I hit him. "For real? It's like fucking contagious. You, that Beni, my little sister. Fuck." He stands too, and reaches for his wallet. "We need to wrap this up." He pulls four hundreds from his wallet and throws them onto the cluttered glass-top coffee table in front of us.

"Thanks."

His eyes are on me as I collect the money.

The next afternoon I head outside with Beni's ladder and my toolbox. Some of the trim along the roofline is coming loose and I need something to do with my hands. Adán is helping me by handing me tools from the box on the ground. I'm on the second-to-top rung when a pickup truck pulls up.

"Hey!" It's Dean, shouting through his open window. Badger is in the truck too.

"Yeah?"

"I shoulda said last night, stay away from my kid." He jabs his finger at me, up on the ladder, so it's clear who he means.

I scramble down and trot over to his window, hoping to quiet him down. "What are you talking about?"

"You and I can do business, but I don't want you ever to talk to Badger again."

"You mean because I'm gay."

The boy sits in the passenger seat folding and unfolding his hands.

"Exactly." Dean's blue eyes are lit up with a belated rage. He's wearing a camo vest over a T-shirt, and for the first time I notice the *88* tattooed on his forearm. Next to it is an Iron Cross. "I'm trying to raise a normal kid here, and I don't need him getting confused by any of your perverted ideas. You got it?"

Instead of answering him, I lean in toward the open window and say, "Hi, Badger!" in my cheeriest voice.

The devil gets the better of me sometimes.

Dean throws the truck into reverse, then drive, making a

tight U-turn half on the road, half in the yard, forcing me to jump out of the way.

"Paula?" Adán approaches, still holding a handful of nails.

"Yeah, bud?"

"Why doesn't he want you to talk to Badger?"

"Because I'm gay. He thinks it's contagious, like the flu." I try to make light of it by laughing, but the laughter sounds fake, even to me.

Adán drops the nails back into the toolbox. "I think there's a lot of people who are gay. I mean, besides you and Mom."

"Sure there are."

He pokes a finger into his cheek like he's thinking something through. "So that means he's probably talking to gay people all the time and he doesn't even know it."

"Yeah, well, I don't think Badger's dad is thinking about it all that hard."

After dinner Beni and Adán want to watch a movie, so I slip out to work on a project in the shed out back.

"Don't come out," I call. "I'm making you something." I'm building Adán a bat house from plans I found on the Internet and some scrap lumber in the shed.

An hour later I set down my saw and step out for some fresh air. The moonless night promises a frost and I rub my stiff legs to warm them.

Across the road, a kid is headed for the ravine that runs down into the woods to the west of the trailer park. He looks over his shoulder as he passes under the streetlight. I check my phone for the time. It's almost ten, late for anyone so small to be out by himself. I go around back of Beni's trailer and the next, to the edge of the trees. The kid disappears over the lip of the ravine. I hear him rustling through dry leaves, then the *clock-clock* of logs being thrown. A few minutes later he emerges, pushing a bicycle.

I jog back to Beni's place and wait against the wall of the trailer that runs beneath her carport. The TV inside is flashing blue and white, casting a chaotic light on the pale gravel. The movie is reaching its climax, full of explosions and people yelling.

The kid, who I can now confirm is Badger, rounds the corner of the trailer. He lets the bike fall to the ground and turns to run, but I collar him and put my hand over his mouth.

His eyes are wide and his neck is sweaty as he wrenches himself away. I don't have the heart to hold a kid long against his will, but I'm pissed.

"Is that Adán's bike?" I ask, even though I know it is. I'd recognize it in a lineup of a hundred bikes, given how much it cost me.

"Yeah." Badger's face crumples and he starts to cry.

"Why'd you take it?"

He's pinching his eyelids to make the tears stop.

"Badger, why'd you take his bike and throw it in the ditch?" I can't keep the anger out of my voice.

"I don't know. I'm sorry! I brought it back, okay?" His voice fills with a rising panic. "He just loved it so much, I just wanted to take it. Don't tell, okay? Okay?"

His fear takes years off him and my fury turns to pity.

"Look, kid. I'm glad you brought the bike back, but I think you should tell Adán what happened. You gotta apologize to him."

He stands frozen, the light from the movie flashing across his face.

"Come on, buddy. I don't think he'll be mad for long. He really likes you, you know."

Badger wipes his face with his shirt, then nods. He's limp, his feet dragging. I half expect he'll reach for my hand as we take the dark steps, but he doesn't.

I open the door and call in, "Hey, Beni, can you turn that off for a minute? Someone's here to see Adán."

Beni gets up from the couch and switches on a lamp in the living room. "Adán, turn the movie off for a sec." When she sees Badger she glances at the clock above the door. "Badger? It's late for a visit, honey."

Adán practically dances over. "Badger!" Then he sees my face. "What's going on?"

"I found your bike," Badger says.

"Badger." I give his arm a quick swat.

He glares at me then drops his gaze to study his shoes. "I took your bike but now I brought it back."

"You did?" Adán goes to the door and looks out. "Yes! Mom! It's here."

Beni leans out the open door to look too. "Why would you do that, Badger?"

He offers only a shake of the head and a shrug.

"Did you want to tell Adán something?" I ask.

Badger sighs like he's been holding his breath. "I'm sorry, Adán. Please don't be mad at me."

Outside there is a crunch of gravel and the door swings wide open, letting in a rush of cold air. Before I can react, Dean is in the room.

"What are you doing to my boy?" He grabs the kid and

yanks the door open wider. "Badger, go wait outside." He turns to me, his finger in my face. "I told you to stay away from my kid."

"You need to get out of here," Beni says. She pulls Adán behind her.

Dean keeps his attention on me. His eyes are red, glazed with a substance—beer or weed or both. "I'm not gonna let you turn my son into a queer." He shoves me. "You dyke. You dirty, cunt-eating dyke." He pushes me again, harder this time, hard enough that I stumble back into the long counter that divides the living room from the kitchen. My knees go weak and it takes a minute for me to catch my footing.

On the counter is a paring knife left over from making dinner. It's short, but it'll do. I grab it as I right myself.

Dean slugs me and I feel a bone give way in my face.

Beni screams and pushes Adán toward his bedroom. "Go!"

The pain in my jaw is like a thousand electric needles. My left eye is filling with stars, but my right eye can see that Dean is drawing back for another blow.

Beni scrambles for her phone.

Before Dean can hit me again, I charge him with the pitiful blade. I go for just under the ribs and it's enough to throw him. He staggers back and I follow him, taking advantage of his backward motion to knock him flat on his ass.

I jump on him, straddling his chest and pinning his arms with my legs. I put the bloody knife to his neck, press the point into the soft skin under his chin.

Dean is still raging, twisting beneath me. "Get off me, you fucking cunt!"

I push the knife in deeper and the skin pops. A drop of red rolls down the blade. "I can press harder, if you want."

He hocks in my face, the phlegm hitting me just under my swelling eye, but he grows still.

Beni's on the phone with the police dispatcher. I don't like the idea of getting the cops involved. If they find out about the weed deal I could go to jail or lose my job. But I also don't know how long I can hold Dean down without killing him. And I don't want to kill him. For my sake, not his. Neo-Nazi fuckhead.

The cops arrest us both for good measure, but after questioning they let me go. Dean goes to the hospital for surgery—something I hope he can't afford—and then to jail to await trial for home invasion. Beni drives me up to the hospital in La Crosse, forty miles away, so Dean and I don't find ourselves in the same small-town emergency room.

At the trial, Adán and Beni are both called as witnesses. Adán does great, backing up my story from the start until the point when his mom sent him to his room. Beni does great too. And apparently Dean keeps quiet about any drug deals. For his sake, no doubt, not mine.

Beni's got to move out of the trailer park. It won't be safe for her and Adán once Dean's out of jail, in eight months to a year, depending on behavior.

Beni makes some noises about the possibility of them coming back to Milwaukee and living with me again, though I don't take the bait. There was a moment just after the fight with Dean that I felt an almost animal urge to be a family again, to nest, but that feeling passed. Now the idea makes me feel trapped.

When Beni gives up, I'm relieved.

"I think it's still better to raise Adán out here in the country anyway," she says. "I'll look for something up the road, in town, where there'll be more people around to keep an eye out."

I can't help but ask Adán to keep tabs on how Badger's doing. He's living with his grandma nearby until Dean gets out, yet I worry about him trying to make it through life with a dad like that. "Maybe you two can keep being friends at school. But, you know, secretly."

"I don't know," Adán says. His little brows draw together in worry, making me feel bad for asking. "His dad was pretty angry."

"I remember." I touch my cheek where the doctor stitched my face back together. I still have all my teeth, but I bet these bones are going to ache when it rains.

"I think I probably shouldn't." He looks at me, searching my face for permission to say no.

The poor kid is trying not to cry, so I let it go.

An Early Specimen

by Elizabeth McCracken

In Italy she was a tourist—that is, she was an animal; that is, she would have gladly ripped out the throat of any other tourist with her teeth. Altogether this was an improvement. As a young woman she would have offered up her own throat instead. *How would you like to die?* a friend had once asked. Her answer: beaten to death by a mob. At least that way your last moments would be made of passion and touch. At least that way you'd know who to blame.

It was hot. Because it was Italy? Because these days everywhere was hot? The lines into museums were full of human suffering. Suffering was fine. It was on her to-do list. She was the opposite of homesick: she didn't wish to feel at home or at ease anywhere in the world. She had become a tourist. She came from nowhere and no history.

Even so, waiting made her furious. She stood in front of the Uffizi in one of the seemingly dozens of lines, all of which followed different grammars. Oh, she hated everyone around her equally—a relief, no nationality more than another, German or Chinese or Swedish or her own countrypeople, the old fool saying to his wife, "Loretta. Loretta. Loretta. Should I take a picture of this?" *This* might have referred to an ancient pillar or the tattered pigeon limping like an old professor on the bricks. Perhaps Loretta's husband took pictures of pigeons wherever he was. They were famous in their subdivision, The Lorettas, for their specialty slideshow: pigeons of the world.

Finally she was let into the gallery, was allowed to pay, was confronted with a vast staircase to climb. There were more stairs in Italy than any other country, she was sure of it. *All right*, she told herself, as she did every time she climbed stairs in Italy, *let us make it a devotion*. She was a tourist; she had no past; but her present was middle-aged and stout. With every step, she vowed, she would cast something away. Problem was, everything she'd ever done made stairs terrible, every cigarette, every gelato, every moment of her sedentary life. What a barbaric way to rise into the air, hauling your own carcass up inches at a time. But there was always something at the top of the stairs to look at, a view or a famous painting, so up she went.

In front of the Uccellos, selfie sticks proliferated and tilted like lances. A wall of people snapping photos blotted out the Botticelli you could buy in the gift shop as a postcard, a poster, an eyeglasses case, a pillbox, a Day-Glo statuette. Famous art made an idiot of everyone.

Her too. These days, the news from everywhere was grim, end-of-the-world, and so any collection of people struck her as a dress rehearsal for the very end of the end, when the bombs dropped and the demons reached up from hell to snag ankles. You'd either be one of the morons photographing the apocalypse, or one of the morons tutting at the morons with the cameras, but Eternity would come for all of you. Eternity or the opposite of it—nothing.

The paintings were in the galleries and the sculptures in

the corridors. At the end of the first corridor she ran into a dark stone sculpture of a she-wolf which had lost its head and its tail and most of its legs and its Romulus and Remus (if it had ever had them) and looked, in fact, like a loaf of pumpernickel with teats. Loretta and her husband had caught up and were taking pictures. He used his phone. She had a plastic disposable camera, with toy plastic grinding gears. *Krk, krk, krk.* "What is that?" Loretta asked Loretta's husband. Loretta wore a red beret that seemed to have fallen from a height onto her head; she was very small, bright-eyed like a bird.

Her husband was large and slack-faced. He said, "Looks like a meatloaf."

"They call it something different here," said Loretta, in an unsettling child's voice, certain and fluty. She added, "When in Rome."

They were not in Rome.

I am a tourist, thought the tourist. They all swam from the same cove, with the same objective. They'd come from Tourismo; they came to look. *I know how you feel*, the tourist thought at the amputated she-wolf. Oh, she had to get out of here. Even inside the Uffizi it was hot, which she imagined was terrible for the art. She felt like alerting the authorities.

She remembered reading about another museum across the river, of wax anatomical models from the eighteenth century. Flayed women and lonely hearts, literal lonely hearts by themselves in glass cabinets, next to the lonely livers and lonely lungs.

A museum of waxworks would have to be kept cool, surely, even in the Old World.

Before she'd come to Italy, she'd been in the woods, but now she was in the jungle, the arms and legs of other people like vines that threatened to wrap around her. She crossed the Ponte Vecchio and paused for not a single photographer hoping to take a picture of a beloved; she strode through and snapped all those little leashes of attention. Too hot to stop. Too crowded. People were quicksand. At the far end of the bridge she stopped for a medically necessary gelato. Frutti di bosco. Small, but this was one of those stands whose small was actually enormous, and expensive, and served with the traditional gelato napkin, so unabsorbent it might as well have been a butter knife. The gelato was delicious and she hated it, hated the man who had handed her the cone, big as Liberty's torch, and demanded five euros. She was still eating it, slurping it, *working on it*, as they said in the country of her past, when she came upon the Palazzo Pitti. She thought, *I have built myself a Pity Palace too.*

It didn't matter where she'd come from, Loretta. Why she thought she might like to see a flayed wax lady. Who was waiting for her or wasn't: an unhappy marriage or one entirely over or a marriage gone slightly green around the edges in the way of cheap jewelry. A friend who'd planned to accompany her but who had instead fallen in love and run off to Alaska. A child. The death of a child. The death of a parent. None of your business.

The courtyard in front of the museum of ancient anatomical wax models—actually the natural history museum—was the first quiet place she'd been in days. In the heat, surrounded by people, everything had seemed like a catastrophe, but now she felt as though she'd walked into a patch of luck. A vending machine stood in the corner, unlikely and glowing, and from it she purchased a bottle of water for sixty cents, if they were called cents, she wasn't sure. It was extraordinarily cold. Her brain, too, cooled and quieted. The museum was on the third and fourth floors. There was an elevator. She took it.

It turned out that wax models were only accessible by guided tour, and no more were offered that day. The tourist used her paltry Italian on the sympathetic young woman at the counter and understood that if she followed around the rest of the museum—a vast collection of taxidermied animals—she would eventually wind around to the wax galleries, and she would be able to peer in on her way out. She bought her admission. No signs of any other visitors, not the most distant footfall.

There were twenty-four rooms of glass cases of stuffed animals in the natural history museum, including a seventeenth-century hippopotamus that had once belonged to the Medici. Born in the seventeenth century, died in the seventeenth century, stuffed in the seventeenth century. The hippo had company. Pangolins, a skunk. A walrus filled to bursting with a long scar down his chest, looking like a heart patient who wouldn't reform his habits despite everything. Two slack-jawed sharks, one a lunatic bon vivant, the other (only a slight turndown in his expression) aghast at his colleague. She felt pressing upon her the heat of every living animal she'd ever known, the bad poodle who bit, the well-intentioned poodle who never was truly housebroken, the neurotic tuxedo cat, the suave ginger tabby.

Once on a walk in Ireland with somebody she'd loved, a tourist there too, they'd been followed by first one dog—a Jack Russell with a notched ear—and then another (a mostly dalmatian), another (a frosted bony mutt), and then it was like a bad musical number, musical because the sun was out and they were near the ocean: in ordinary Irish light it might have seemed like a horror movie. Dog after dog. A dog-walking club. No, you couldn't keep animals out, she thought, and then a little voice said, "Oh, they killed somebody's guinea pig."

The speaker was a small girl, peering into a cabinet. The tourist hadn't caught her accent, though it didn't sound American.

"Perhaps it died of natural causes," said the tourist.

The girl turned. She was very pretty in the way of bad art, with tears in her dark eyes and a flush across her cheeks, black-haired and copper-skinned. Bad art and not good because of the tears, and the tragic look. There was a message here. Suffer the children, or something.

"I don't like places like this," said the girl. Her voice was hollow-throated. Younger children loved museums of natural history—not because they didn't understand that the animals were dead, but because they did not yet understand that it was possible, perhaps even essential, to blame somebody for this fact. This girl had grown past that stage, was eight, perhaps. The guinea pig was roan and unkempt.

"Nobody killed the guinea pig," said the tourist to the guinea pig, then added, "It would have died by now anyhow." She turned and the girl was gone, as if a ghost. Bad work for a ghost, to haunt twenty-four rooms of dead animals. Her parents must have been ahead.

The tourist walked past the wall of birds, perhaps two hundred standing on their perches. Past fish, for whom she felt nothing. A stoat, whom she loved. A capybara. Mice. The rooms were warm, for a museum, but tolerable.

She was surprised to take pleasure in the animals. She was surprised to take pleasure in anything.

Then she turned the corner and saw two chimpanzees, and the pleasure was over. Ah, no. It was wrong to display primates. She believed that. It was like mummies in the museum, you could forget for a moment that they were the bodies of somebody's child, or mother, put in a glass case for you to gawk at. But then, if you were a good person, you remembered. One chimpanzee squatted on the floor of its case and lifted a languid hand and gestured at the next door case which held—

—a woman.

Undeniably a woman, alive, in a caftan with a scruffy orange metallic pattern, and sunglasses, the kind that had been popular in the eighties, with doglegged arms and a pair of tiny initials stuck to the bottom right lens. She held her hands up as though roaring. Her head was huge, and her hair a dozen artificial colors: a skein of orangey red, skeins of store-bought caramel, lemon drop, lemon cake, Atomic Fireball. The woman seemed to notice the tourist. Then she stepped from the case—there was an exit right there, with three steps down—and said, in a hollow-throated accent, "Oh good, it's you."

The tourist looked over her shoulder, for the little girl to whom the woman must have been speaking. She wasn't there.

"You understand," said the woman. She pointed at the case. Behind it was a mirror. "So you can see how it feels. For the children and for the suffering."

The tourist could make no sense of anything. The woman was monstrous and glamorous, illustrated how close monstrosity and glamor really were. She did not taper in any of the places you might expect a woman to taper, not at the wrist or ankles, not her fingers, not her waist or neck. One part of her simply arrived at the next. In all of these intersections she wore jewelry as though to either camouflage or call attention. Her bangles chimed. Her belt gleamed.

She flipped her glasses up to reveal a pair of bottle-green eyes. "Did you hear a child?" she asked.

The tourist pointed behind her. "She's there."

The woman nodded distractedly. She settled her sunglasses into her variegated hair. Then she looped her arm through the tourist's, the stacks of bangles chittering as she locked her elbow down. It hurt. The tourist wondered whether to struggle. It was strange place to have a hand trapped, her knuckles against the woman's breast, which was encased in a brassiere of immense power: she could nearly feel the cabbage roses in the weave. Why wear a caftan and such serious underwear?

"You have seen the elephant," the monstrous, glamorous woman said.

Had she? The animals of the museum felt like a dream that was starting to break into pieces. Noah's Ark in a house of mirrors; Noah's Ark at the bottom of the sea.

"I don't think so."

"You cannot forget the elephant." The woman looked over the tourist's head, and said again, "Ah, good. It's you."

There was the little girl, coming past a case filled with doleful little monkeys, sweet as putti, mere bystanders to the larger disaster but blessed just the same. The girl looked smudged and wild now, a feral child raised by wolves who'd just happened to be stuffed and mounted. No way would she surrender herself to a living human being. She paused in front of the monkeys and said, "It's like they're in jail."

"It is not," said the woman.

The girl put her hand to the glass of the monkey case. "How do you know?"

"Because I have been in jail."

"But have you been a monkey?" said the little girl, and the woman laughed. She spread her arms out and dropped the tourist's hand, a seashell and now here was a better seashell. But the girl put her cheek to the glass, next to her hand. She did not budge.

"You want to live forever in the museum?" the woman asked. "You want to sleep among the monkeys?"

"The birds," said the girl. "Yes."

"They have lost their habitat," said the woman, "and so have I. La Specola," said the woman to the tourist. "They call this museum so."

"That means—*the mirror*?" asked the tourist. Her dropped hand felt sore and cold. She caught it up with the other hand, and held it like a damaged bird.

"*The observatory*," said the woman. She gestured to the heavens. "There used to be one. Up top. The elephant is a woman. You cannot forget her."

"Beg pardon?" said the tourist.

"They have only her skeleton. Her name is Hansken. She was born in Ceylon. Rembrandt knew her. Knew her and drew her. She was educated, our Hansken, could draw a sword and such tricks. An Asian elephant. Little ears, that's the difference. They have lost her skin and so they show the bones. She traveled the world. It seems impossible, does it not, for so large and ponderous a creature to come from Ceylon to Holland, from Holland to Italy."

Which place had once been Ceylon? The tourist was embarrassed to have forgotten. An Asian elephant: somewhere in Asia. She looked at the woman and at the girl, trying to find a family resemblance, and then she began to worry.

"Who are you?" she asked the woman.

"Call me Hansken."

"She's your granddaughter."

"Is that what you think?" the woman said, amused. "Come."

They turned the corner into a long corridor. Doorways along the hallway were garlanded by velvet ropes, blocking the way, but beyond the ropes were the waxworks. She could see in one glass case a wax woman reclining, slit down the middle to display her wax viscera.

"Hello, friend," the monstrous woman said, and the tourist turned to her, but the woman was addressing a skeleton, a human one, which stood behind glass in the corridor. The skeleton was immense. A giant. "Bones made of wax," said the woman. "Made by Clemente Susini. A friend of the giant. His bones are in a crypt, and here are his counterfeit bones. When he was done making them, the artist was so pleased he decided he would sign his work, but in a place nobody would see. So he signed the inside of the skull. Some days I feel like that."

"Pleased?"

"You misunderstand everything. As though some man has signed the inside of my skull." The woman put her strange hand to one of the velvet ropes. "We could, you know. We could just—"

"No thank you," said the tourist.

"Hop over."

"No," said the tourist, though truthfully she always wanted to misbehave in museums. To touch the she-wolf's udders, to lick the bare feet of Venus. Was this misbehavior? She still thought, hoped, the woman worked here.

"You then," the woman said to the girl, who shook her head. "No? You are too good."

"You then," said the tourist.

"Ah, no," said the woman. "Myself, I cannot risk it. Because I am not good. Darling one," she said to the little girl, "I suppose it is time for you to go home."

The tourist had been for weeks attuned to danger. She was a tourist, after all, a mark, a rube, what did it matter if she were cheated, it harmed nothing but her pride, but pride was the primary thing she'd packed from home. You had to suspect everyone. Now she remembered. Was she witnessing a kidnapping? An attempted kidnapping, if she intervened. What was worse, to watch a child taken away by a stranger, or to accuse a stranger of unspeakable intent? She knew the answer, but she knew which she'd rather do.

"She died in Florence," said the woman. "Hansken. She was flayed in the Boboli Gardens. And now her skeleton is here. That is what happens when you travel. Your bones may end up anywhere. Your very bones. We must go. Come," she said to the girl.

"Whose child is this?" asked the tourist.

The woman ruffled the girl's hair. Then she took the girl's hand. A sign, oh good, they belonged together. Then again, she had taken the tourist's hand. "Whose indeed?" said the woman. "You will come with us? You may, you know."

Then the lights went off, down the long corridor one at a time, and in this way it did not seem like a catastrophe, but as though the museum were falling asleep by degrees. Nothing so dire as to hurry them. Still, by the time they got to the lobby, the young woman at the counter was gone and the doors locked from the outside. They had been forgotten.

"Why are you waving?" the woman asked the tourist.

"Motion detectors."

"Not every place has the things you believe are necessary. Most days," said the woman, leaning back, "I am not the giant man. Most days I am the elephant. You understand."

An unwilling immigrant, forced to stand near the site of her flaying. A familiar story.

The girl's shoulders had puffed up in the dark, as was typical of her species. The glass in the door made them feel as taxidermied as the animals, shaggy, moth-eaten, with store-bought eyes.

"It's all right, beauty," the woman said to the tourist, or the girl, or both. "We can last here a long time."

OBF, Inc.

by Bernice L. McFadden

Andrew was entering his third month of unemployment when he sat down at his computer and opened the inbox of his LinkedIn account. He'd received a response to a query he'd sent off four days after his friend-turned-manager walked him into a conference room swimming with sunlight, smelling of cologne and the faintest hint of perfume left behind by a group of attorneys who'd recently vacated the space after a five-hour meeting.

"I'm sorry, man," Colin Perkins had said. Andrew's eyes glided to the glass conference table, landing on the silver tray holding a molehill of bagels. He imagined they must be stale by now, having been left there uncovered in the icy office air.

Someone had planted the pointed end of a white plastic knife in an open container of chive-and-jalapeño cream cheese. It brought to mind the moon landing; all that was missing was a tiny American flag. A laugh trudged up his throat, but he disguised it as a cough.

"I told you," Colin continued, raking his hands over his manicured Afro, "that the last to hire would be the first to go."

A month earlier, seventeen women and two men had accused the CEO of the company of sexual misconduct. That news had plummeted the stock. The layoffs followed. Andrew had witnessed dozens of employees being escorted by security from the building like criminals. Now it was his turn.

Andrew nodded, placed a comforting hand on Daniel's shoulder, and squeezed. The crisp cotton of Daniel's shirt felt cool beneath his palm. "It's okay, man, I understand. Don't sweat it."

He'd spent that first week revamping his résumé, calling friends and old colleagues, people who might know of a job opportunity at their own place of employment or elsewhere. He'd never had a LinkedIn account, but took the time to set one up. To conserve the little bit of savings he had, Andrew dropped his gym membership and went back to drinking tap water instead of the bottled Evian he loved. He gave up Starbucks coffee and the expensive cabernet sauvignon he purchased by the case.

By week three, he was spending his days on the couch, dressed in boxer shorts and sweat socks. He'd stopped opening the blinds and only went outside to empty the garbage. He whiled away the hours playing video games, and watching Netflix and Pornhub. Oftentimes, he went days without brushing his teeth.

When his mother called to check on him, Andrew lied, claiming he had several interviews lined up. When his father took the phone into another room to ask if he needed money, Andrew assured him that he was fine on the financial front, even though he wasn't. He'd made up his mind to sell his Shelby Mustang before he took a dime from his parents. That was a big decision because he loved that car more than he'd ever loved any woman.

The day he opened the e-mail, the panic had just started to set in. He could feel it creeping along the back of his neck, like the soft scuttle of caterpillar legs.

From: OBF, INC.
To: Andrew Jamison

Dear Mr. Jamison,
We found your resume to be very interesting and believe that you would be the perfect addition to our dynamic team of Client Liaisons.

PAID TRAINING!

Affordable benefits for you, your spouse, and/or children after 90 days!

Opportunities to advance within!

Hourly, overtime, and tremendous bonus opportunities!

If you love helping others, then you will love working for OBF, INC.

OBF, INC. wants to talk to you now! To set up an interview TEXT OBF51893.

Liaison was just a fancy French word for *customer service agent.* Well, that was his skill set. Andrew was an expert at assisting people.

He texted the number and received an instant response that directed him to call a telephone number and enter his personal code: 1032.

An automated voice offered him two available interview dates. He was instructed to press 1 for the first date and 2 for the second. The mechanical voice told him that he would receive a call advising him where the interview would take place.

It all seemed very clandestine. Andrew was cynical, but his desperation outweighed his skepticism.

A day later, he received a call from a woman with a Southern drawl . . . Georgia, Alabama, Texas? He couldn't quite pinpoint where she hailed from, but listening to her speak conjured visions of sweet tea and fireflies. She asked for his full government name and the code he'd received via text message. There was a pause, two clicks, and then the syrupy voice asked if he had a pen available. He did. After she'd rattled off the address, she wished him good luck. There were a few more clicks and then the line went dead.

He walked into the lobby of the forty-story office building and was struck by the contemporary opulence of the space. Marble floors, potted palms that towered eight feet into the air, white leather sofas, and a slick-looking Louboutin-red reception desk.

Andrew presented his license to the security guard and was given a name tag, which he clipped to the lapel of his ash-gray jacket. He was told to go to the eighteenth floor.

While waiting for the elevator, he perused the list of companies listed on a plaque mounted to the wall. OBF, Inc. was nowhere to be found.

He smirked, shrugged his shoulders, and stepped into the elevator. On the eighteenth floor, smack outside of the elevator door, was a sheet of lined legal paper taped haphazardly to the wall. Scrawled on its face in black marker was: *This Way to OBF, INC*. Below that was an arrow.

He started down the hall. A man the color of cedar and as tall as an NBA player speed-walked past him, mumbling to himself. Andrew thought he looked dazed, as if he'd just received news that a loved one had passed away.

"Good morning," Andrew murmured.

The man turned eyes as wide as saucers on Andrew. He opened his mouth and muttered something that Andrew wasn't sure he'd heard correctly. The elevator doors slid open just as Andrew leaned in and asked, "Uhm, sorry, brother, but did you say *run*?"

The man leaped into the elevator, pressed his spine against the back wall, and fixed his eyes on the glass numbers above the closing doors.

Andrew stood blinking at his reflection in the chrome elevator doors. After a moment, he shrugged and continued down the hallway where he came upon a second handwritten sign directing him to turn left at the women's bathroom. He rounded a corner and found himself staring at eleven men seated in folding chairs. They all looked up from their iPhones and Androids. Andrew nodded and headed toward the pretty blonde seated behind a metal desk.

"Good morning," she smiled. "Name?"

"Andrew Jamison."

"Okay, Mr. Jamison, please take a seat. Mrs. Americus will be with you shortly."

He scrutinized his fellow applicants. They were all black men save for the one white guy with a man-bun who was called in as soon as Andrew sat down. Man-bun wasn't in there long. In less than five minutes, cheeks flushed and cursing under his breath, he stormed across the reception area and out of sight.

Andrew clenched his jaw and made eye contact with another man across the room from him. He imagined the unease in the man's eyes mirrored his own uncertainty.

"Andrew Jamison, Mrs. Americus will see you now. Just through that door."

The door opened to a large office filled with cubicles and desks, manned by women tapping away on typewriters or murmuring into the handsets of—

Andrew slowed his gait.

Are those rotary telephones and, wait, Royal typewriters?

As Andrew gawked, a large man with a mustache as thick has a shoe brush appeared before him. Andrew glanced up and then quickly shifted his gaze away from the brawny man's left eyelid, which was weighed down with a sty the size of a dime.

"In there," the man huffed, aiming a chubby finger at a closed door not more than five feet from where they stood.

The office was as small as a janitor's closet. And dark.

The lone window on the far left wall faced the shadowy back of a department store. Metal file cabinets lined the walls; some of the drawers were open, revealing manila folders bulging with papers. He could see, even in the muddy darkness of the room, a layer of dust atop the cabinets. Hanging on the walls were at least twenty framed photographs of people, all of whom were black.

The air was rife with the scent of cigarette smoke.

Andrew remembered people smoking at their desks when he went to visit his mother at her office job when he was young. Once, on a flight to Detroit with his grandmother, he stood at the back of the plane waiting to use the bathroom, and found himself engulfed in a cloud of smoke billowing from the cigarettes of three passengers.

He couldn't recall the exact year cities around the country began banning smoking in bars and restaurants, but he was supremely aware that smokers had to be at least four hundred feet away from the entrance of any building if they wanted to light up.

Yet here was this woman, puffing away like it was 1975. Andrew eyed the near-empty box of Winstons and then the woman. She was robust—a meat-and-potatoes sort of gal, with doughy cheeks and large blue eyes. Her sun-bleached blond hair fanned back from her face—a style made famous by the eighties icon Farrah Fawcett. Her lips were slathered in tangerine-colored lipstick. The same color rung the filters of a dozen long-dead Winston butts heaped in the black ceramic ashtray. Andrew thought, *If she's going for clown instead of glamour, well, bull's-eye!*

Ornate rings twinkled on seven of her ten fingers, the rose-gold chain she wore around her neck dribbled down her chest and disappeared into her cleavage. She looked to be in her midfifties.

"Good morning, Mr. Jamison. Please have a seat." Her eyes remained glued to the sheet of paper clutched in her hands. Andrew assumed it was his résumé.

He sat down.

"You graduated from Brown University?"

"Y-yes, I did. I graduated summa cum laude in 1990."

Her desk was cluttered with newspaper clippings; stacks of aging yellowed papers, and dated fashion magazines. Andrew's eyebrows climbed. Was that Marcia from the seventies sitcom *The Brady Bunch* on the cover of that *Glamour* magazine?

Andrew chuckled to himself. This had to be an elaborate joke. Someone was putting him on. His eyes ranged around the office in search of a concealed camera.

"Impressive," she said finally, looking him directly in the eye. "Do you have a wife?"

"S-sorry?"

"Are you married, Mr. Jamison?"

"No, I'm not."

She searched his face. "Are you gay?"

Andrew bristled. "Mrs. Americus, I don't think you're legally allowed to ask me that question."

She smirked.

"It's a yes-or-no question, Mr. Jamison. I know it's unusual, but believe me, for this position I would need to know."

His rent was due tomorrow and then again in thirty more days. His savings were dwindling. "No, I'm not gay."

"Do you have children?"

"One daughter, she's twenty-two years old."

"Do you have a good relationship with your daughter? With the mother?"

"Yes."

Mrs. Americus glanced at his résumé. "Perfect." She reached for the dying cigarette and brought it to her lips. "And according to your application, you've never been arrested. Is that true?"

"Yes."

"Well, we will be doing a background check."

"Understood."

"Do you have any bad habits? Do you use narcotics?"

"No ma'am."

"Any . . . um . . . undesirable recreational activities?"

"Undesirable?"

"Porn? Well, not just porn. Kiddie porn."

Andrew's mouth fell open.

"No judgment, Mr. Jamison. Again, I just need to know."

"No, I do not watch kiddie porn," Andrew spat.

"Good!" she exclaimed, drumming her fingers on the desk. "Let me tell you the specifics of the job . . ."

Some of the faces behind the glass frames looked familiar. Again Andrew found himself squinting. Was that Omarosa? He pitched forward in his chair.

Mrs. Americus stopped talking and followed his gaze. "Um, yes," she spouted. "That is who you think it is. She's been one of our best recruits."

Andrew swallowed.

Mrs. Americus stubbed out her cigarette and laced her fingers under her chin. "Some of our liaisons work directly with government agencies. That's a promotion of sorts. Of course, before you can be assigned to the big house—I mean the White House—you'd first have to prove yourself out in the field." She giggled. "*In the field.* You get it? It's a double entendre."

Andrew's mouth went dry.

She twisted around in the chair and pointed to a photograph of a pair of middle-aged women standing shoulder to shoulder, each holding a red *MAGA* baseball cap. "Those ladies are Diamond and Silk. Do you know them?"

Andrew shot out up from the chair. For a moment, he thought his knees would buckle. "What does OBF stand for?"

Mrs. Americus reached for the pack of cigarettes. "OBF stands for One Black Friend."

"One Black Friend?"

"Yes. You see, in these troubling times, times where so many people are labeling white people as racist, we need black people to stand up for us—to have our backs, as your people are fond of saying. Sometimes, Mr. Jamison, a God-fearing, good white person may be accused of a crime or some other offense perpetrated against a person of color, and when the accused does not have a person of color in his circle, it looks bad. The public may see him . . . or her, as a racist simply because their circle is . . . white. Lily.

"And that's wrong. Not having black friends does not make a white person racist by default. Anyway," she waved her hand, "that's where OBF comes in. We provide that one black friend. That one black friend introduces doubt, and more often than not, that doubt diminishes a large percentage of the negative impact our clients might face."

Andrew just stared.

"Oh, Mr. Jamison, don't look so shocked. This practice has been around for centuries." She pointed to the far wall near the window. "You see that guy there? He was actually the inspiration for this company."

Andrew peered at the photograph. "Who is he?"

"Joe Oliver."

"Joe Oliver?"

"Yeah, Joe Oliver. You don't remember him? Joe Oliver, George Zimmerman's one black friend." Mrs. Americus raised a black ceramic coffee mug to her lips and sipped. The red decal on the side of the mug read: *Black Tears*.

Andrew's stomach lurched, perspiration beading across his forehead. "This is some kind of joke, right?"

"Oh, I assure you this is not a joke and I am very serious.

As serious as a heart attack. Is that how the saying goes? *As serious as a heart attack?*"

Andrew started toward the door.

"Wait, Mr. Jamison. Look here." She pointed at a photograph hanging above the row of filing cabinets. "This is another one of our liaisons. Since he's been working for us, he's paid off his student loans and I understand that he's just recently purchased a Cadillac."

Andrew followed her index finger to the photo of a grinning black man holding a *Blacks for Trump* sign above his head like a trophy.

"Shall we talk about salary?"

The lights flickered.

He thought, *Maybe I'm still asleep. Maybe this is a nightmare.*

"Andrew? I can see you're having a hard time processing all of this. But really, it's not as uncommon as you might think. We live in America, this is a capitalist country, and we monetize everything. *Everything.*"

Andrew couldn't remember reaching for the doorknob, but suddenly he was stumbling through the reception area.

He fled down the corridor, rounded the first corner and then the next. A slight man the color of honeyed milk stepped from the elevator. He wore a yellow dress shirt with a red bow tie. His dark-blue khakis were flooded just enough to offer a wink of his orange-and-navy argyle socks.

Upon Andrew's frantic approach, the startled stranger stepped swiftly out of his path. Andrew didn't make eye contact. He jabbed at the elevator button until the doors slid open.

Weeks later, Andrew was seated in a truck-stop diner with his fork poised over a plate of scrambled eggs and corned beef hash.

The mounted television was tuned to Fox News. The anchor reported that yet another young black man had been gunned down by a vigilante, another Good Samaritan, named Christopher Parks.

Christopher Parks was heading home from his job as a sanitation man when he spotted young Daniel Latham sitting in Starbucks, dozing over his law textbooks. Parks entered the establishment, woke Latham with a tap to his shoulder, and asked if he lived in the area. According to eyewitnesses, Latham replied that he did in fact live in the neighborhood. Parks demanded to see Latham's ID and was met with laughter. The law student gathered his belongings and stood to leave—rather menacingly, one eyewitness reported.

That was when Christopher Parks pulled his weapon and fired. The stunned Latham, still laughing, crumpled into his chair and pressed his hand over the whole in his heart. It wasn't until he saw the blood that the smile slipped from his lips and he began to cry.

The cops were called, but not an ambulance. Well, not immediately.

The police shackled Latham to the chair and took Parks to the police station for questioning. The woman behind the counter gave Parks a high five and a tall Caffè Mocha to go.

By the time an ambulance arrived, Daniel Latham was dead, having bled out all over his take-home final exam.

In the days that followed, it was revealed that Daniel Latham had several unpaid parking tickets and was thrice fined for not scooping his dog's poop. Not only that—he was also a practicing Buddhist who supported a woman's right to choose.

A search of Latham's apartment unearthed a well-worn copy of Alex Haley's *The Autobiography of Malcolm X*, which was on his nightstand alongside Jay-Z's *Decoded*. This discovery was further evidence that Latham was no angel.

Laura Ingraham looked directly into the camera and told her viewers that Christopher Parks was a hero, a polite and well-spoken man who had been raised by his father after his mother died from breast cancer when he was just three years old. Yes, as a youth, Christopher had been suspended from school for fighting, and as a young man he'd beaten a girlfriend with a pipe. Later, when he was in his early thirties, he'd threatened to castrate his boss—a black man old enough to be his grandfather. All of that behavior, Laura Ingraham said, was directly connected to the trauma of losing a mother at such a tender age.

She paused, and in that moment her entire face pulsed with empathy. *"That said,"* she continued, *"Al Sharpton, along with the Black Lives Matter terrorist organization, have labeled Christopher Parks a racist and are calling for his arrest."* She shook her head and chuckled. *"Earlier today, I had the pleasure of speaking with Christopher's longtime best friend, Andrew Jamison . . ."*

Andrew lowered his fork, reached for his shades, and slipped them onto his face.

Firetown

by Aimee Bender

I t had not rained for eleven months. They had predicted El Niño, and then they had predicted a pressure front from the east, but both things had rerouted so that somewhere deep in the ocean, water had fallen onto water.

Instead, Los Angeles was crackling, and again the wildfires were happening one after the other; since last year had actually been rainy, the foliage had grown and then dried and then crisped into the most perfect of kindling.

So when she came into my office, it was not a rainy evening, as it had been so many decades earlier, when my forefathers had their offices in Hollywood, as I had chosen for mine, though mine being by necessity in the basement of the cylindrical Capitol Records building. It was thick and hot, and there was a new wildfire started by an arsonist by Mount Wilson again and they had evacuated the area around the Hubble Telescopes. The sky was gray, tinged with brown. It was ominous, yes, but for the whole world now.

And despite the ever-looming apocalypse, I still have to pay my bills. For now, the city stands. I have made it as easy on myself as possible: the basement office in the Capitol Records building is nearly rent-free, which means it doubles as my apartment, because the PI job has not paid regularly enough to afford me rent in a place more central. In Hollywood alone, a one-bedroom goes for fifteen hundred at least. I shower at the gym, and sleep on the pull-out couch in the office corner. Security is also located down here, a few doors away, so I feel safe. Still, work is key, and work is scarce, and when she arrived, she was wearing clothes that speak of money, clothes whose only job was to telegraph the spending of money. They did look nice on her, but not nicer than similar clothes of less money. They had a smell on them too—not perfume, but almost of receipts, of the faint print residue aroma of credit card machines.

She settled herself wealthily in the one chair I have, the one reserved for clients. Leather, apricot-colored, with an effective leaning-back. I perched on a stool behind the desk, which I found secondhand at Out of the Closet on Santa Monica Boulevard for seven dollars.

"Melanie gave me your name," she said, pulling out a gray tube. She began vaping. "May I?"

"Of course. Melanie is a delight," I said.

"We attend the same spin class."

"She's my cousin," I confessed.

She released a stream of vapor into the air. "Well, I am here because of my cat."

"Your cat?"

"It's lost." She smiled at me.

"Most people do not refer to pets about whom they care as *it*," I said.

She nodded, tapping a fingernail on the tube. "You're attentive," she said. "Good. That's good. And you're right, of course. It's not really about my cat."

"So then why are you here?"

"Because the cat was with my roommate, and they are lost together."

I looked at her, thinking. She let out another stream of vapor that rose up to the ceiling, which is low, speckled by brown water stains.

"You tell me your roommate is lost by attaching him—is it a him?—to the cat, which is also lost?"

"He's really my husband." Her eyes narrowed, and she held her smile, which was turning colder and sharper-edged by the minute.

"He is your husband," I said. "But you call him your roommate."

"I am interested in terminology," she said, leaning in. "And in roundabout information."

"I can see that."

"Can you find him?"

"Your husband?"

"Mmm."

"I can certainly try."

"Please," she said. "Money is no problem. And I don't need you to bring him home, okay? I just need you to find him. I can take it from there."

She stood, and her pants fell back into place instantly, immediately adjusting to her stance.

"What is his name?"

She handed me a card with a sky-blue background and her name printed sans serif in white, *Chelsea DeVeau*, and then she told me the rest was up to me.

Before I began googling the man, and where he worked, and

where she lived, and checking the various databases I pay for to obtain access to exactly this kind of information, I went to sit in the apricot leather chair to consider what had just happened. A woman had come in the door with the information in her mind that her husband had disappeared, but she hid it twice from me, once through the cat, and again through the roommate, although everything she said was true: he did have a cat, and he was, in a way, her roommate. She liked leading me in, and surprising me, and keeping herself almost clean in the process. But it left the listener, me, with a feeling of what I might call granular annoyance. The one thing I bring to my practice that is specific to me beyond regular sleuthing abilities is that I do have a solid sense of right and wrong. Meaning, I have a gauge inside me that will not be manipulated. My mother always called it my precious little North Star because it irritated her, but I never cared that she was irritated. Simply this, and perhaps it would be apparent to you as well: the woman was beautiful, and she presented her twists as clever, as charming, even, to tell me the information in her roundabout way, and I liked looking at her, and talking to her, but what it gave to me most was a sense of disturbance, of a woman so deeply disconnected from her spouse that she first turned him into a cat, and then a roommate. It bothered me. What presents as cuteness can sometimes—often—be a contortion to gain entry to something else. This is why it is often a nightmare to be attracted to anyone and why I make it a policy for myself to go out at least once a week to Jorge's on Vine and make sure to flirt with someone I do not find attractive, who does not light up my meter, who seems entirely ordinary, who may even be nice-looking, but not in a way that I find at all interesting. In this way I have met several terrific people who do not at all register on my own baggage and have been, to my surprise, quite wonderful in bed! One I went along with for many months, but we split up mainly because I work better when single and he was moving, anyway, to Alaska.

The husband, a Mr. Harris DeVeau, worked at a corporation that made global tech connections easier to meet up or something along those lines, something impossible to understand, and he traveled between two offices, one in Santa Monica and another in Downtown LA near the courthouses. I called his Downtown office and when I asked to speak with him heard he was not in today, and when I asked if he had been seen yesterday, the secretary freely told me yes, indeed, he had, and what was I, a private detective? She was chewing gum. I laughed. Millennials are so awkward on the phone. If he had left at five p.m. last night then that was where I would begin, and I decided to take the bus to the Downtown office because I have found that bus rides in Los Angeles deliver clues unexpectedly in a way that a car ride never can, because one is absorbed in a podcast or NPR or KROQ or whatever is one's choice of entertainment to block out the existence of an outside world. I also wanted to feel a sense of civil solidarity during the fires. To comment on the smoke smell, to shake our heads together. The number 2 would take me down Sunset to where it turned into Cesar Chavez and then down 1st near his office. I punched the time clock, my own, a relic, a gesture toward the elders, and began the search for Mr. DeVeau.

The bus ride was uneventful, except for a few gratifying head nods about the weather, the child playing excessive video games and getting a scolding from his grandmother, and the four men in scrubs talking about massage techniques which I found comforting.

In the office, the millennial was packing up.

"I'm looking for Mr. DeVeau," I said.

She squinted at me. "Did you call earlier?"

"No."

"I recognize your voice."

"Did he come in today?"

"No," she said. "You ARE a private dick, aren't you?" She grinned at me.

"Or," I said, "the opposite," and we beamed at each other in what could only be called flirting. "Listen, any clues you can give me would be great. I'll buy you a drink. Downstairs?"

She looked at me, assessed me in some way, and then nodded.

We went downstairs to the Freeway Grill, currently famous for its plates made out of old headlights, and she ordered a summer pale ale, and I had a whiskey, rocks, to maintain image. She told me he had not come in today, and when he had left yesterday he had been distressed. "Not in his usual stressed way," she said, sipping her beer. She looked so sweet, so pink-cheeked, and unexpectedly lovely in the lighting of the bar, with a halo of gold above her from the fixture. I asked her what she really wanted to be, and she told me she was developing her own Etsy site of homemade jewelry and I might look good in some of the hoops. "They're small," she added matter-of-factly.

"Anyway, he's always stressed, but it's like this high-strung stress, and this was all inside, like this quiet personal stress, and that's when he left."

"Did he mention a cat?"

She shook her head. "No. No cat. Is Chewie missing?"

"I can't reveal the details of the case," I said.

"Well, I'll be in tomorrow." She ordered another beer. I bit down on the whiskey ice.

"Shall we go to bed?" I said, and she said yes, that sounded nice, and I followed her home.

I left by eleven p.m., after a fine time, and told her I'd likely see her soon. She asked, tucked in under her floral comforter, hair spread woozily over the pillow, if she was supposed to keep anything secret, but I don't believe in that unless absolutely necessary, so I told her no. She asked if I needed a secretary, as she yawned, ready to doze off, and I told her no, I wasn't a large operation, but that I would certainly be interested in looking at her hoops at a later point.

"They'd look good on you," she said, eyes fluttering closed.

The bus ride home was uneventful again except for the man yelling at the driver to stop at a stop that was not a stop, and the driver stoically continuing to drive forward. Although the news said the fires had recently been contained, the air still smelled strongly of smoke, though everyone seemed tired and done and no one mentioned it.

Back at home, after waving to the security guards, who were leaning back in their chairs, watching the computer monitor video screens, I made myself a cup of peppermint tea on the hot pot. About what was DeVeau distressed? I sipped, and thought, and set my alarm for five a.m., to return to the office or to visit his home, but when the alarm went off, I rolled on my side and fell asleep for four more hours.

Which was good, actually, because the woman, the wife, was knocking on my door by ten, after I'd showered and dressed and was ready to go out into the world.

"I hear you slept with Anna," she said, settling back into the apricot chair.

"That's so unusually direct of you," I said.

She smiled at me. "I heard on the telephone."

"You were listening to a phone call?"

"On the telephone with the secretary. This morning. She told me."

"Are you also sleeping with her?"

She blew her smoke into the air. "You flatter me," she said.

I didn't know what that meant, as the woman was beautiful, and charming, but I didn't feel like asking.

"I'm about to head out," I said, shouldering my backpack. "Any new information?"

She reapplied her lipstick, a dark red, bold for summer, and I noticed her hoops then: thick, gold.

"Well, he's back," she said.

I sat back down on my stool. "Your roommate?"

"And the cat. They're both back."

"Where did they go?"

"He said they went to Santa Barbara for the day to get away from the wildfires."

"There are plenty of fires up there too."

"That's what I told him."

"And he took the cat?"

She shrugged. "I'm just reporting what I heard."

I pulled out a sheet of paper and began adding up my hours.

"But I still want to know *why* he was upset," the woman said. "Anna told me he was distressed. That it was different than his usual stress."

"Ah."

"We are very close," she said, simpering into her collar.

"Is she your daughter?" I asked, trying to assess age, adding possible ages in my head.

"Niece," said Mrs. DeVeau.

"Why don't I go speak to him? He's at work?"

"Of course," she said. "He's always at work. He is made of work."

"And do you work?" I asked.

"No. I prefer to embody the era of my parents. I have no interest in working."

But one look in her eyes spoke of something else—she had ambition; it was as lit in her pupils as the nicotine coursing through her bloodstream. She was a woman with unexpressed drive, but she was in the right era, now, one where she could express it, and so it was confusing. She was continually confusing to me.

I made an appointment with the mister for one p.m., telling him I was a client, and when I entered, and nodded at Anna, who smiled beguilingly at me, I was wearing my best suit, apricot-colored in a tribute to my chair, and when I went inside I explained to him right away why I was there, and that perhaps he might be willing to share with me what had been the source of his distress. I explained that I would not tell his wife exactly what he told me; I would translate it into a way I thought she could digest that would also protect his privacy.

He tapped his hands on the tabletop, and piles of paper framed him, and he stared out past my head for a while, and then gave me an almost imperceptible nod.

"When I was a boy," he said, leaning back in his own rolly chair, "I loved cats. I only wanted to play with my cat. Jet. A black cat. I looked forward all day at school to running home and petting Jet, and Jet knew me and loved me and slept on my head, and one day he slipped out the side door to explore the world and was not able to find his way home again. I do not think Jet did not love me," he said, shaking his head. He looked at the window, at the skyline of Downtown. "But Jet never did return.

"The cat I have with my wife is not a friendly cat, and I was distressed that day because I realized that cat, Chewie, actually did not love me and somehow in that realization I was able to extend the notion to people and understand that neither did she. It has taken me a long time to grasp this. For many years I thought it was just her nature, her reticence, that the love was deep down in there but just not readily visible, but now I think she is either not capable of love, or she simply does not love me, and the cat truly seems to act as an extension of her, because it seems to like being around her even though I don't think it loves her either, nor she it. So I took it somewhere and let it go. I wanted to redo the experience with Jet, to make a deliberate goodbye with this cat. It was practice for divorce. I took it to an area that seemed to be amiable to the cat, one riddled with mice. The cat ran off right away, and I felt it was my first attempt to try to figure out my next step. I cannot make her love me, says the song, and the song is correct.

"But by the time I came home last night, the cat was back." He looked at me, and for that moment, his eyes glittered up with tears. "Odd, right? The cat who does not love us. Or loves us in such a way that we cannot understand its love. It loves in another language, perhaps. There it was, on our stoop, roughed up, with fur pulled out of its eye socket, and a whisker bent, sitting there grooming itself, and it limped back inside, as did I.

"My wife was in the kitchen. She saw the cat and set out food and water and tended to it in a functional way, and even smoothed down the matted fur on its back, and we knew as it settled in that it would deeply groom itself as only cats know how to do. Love or no love, we were a place of safety and nourishment. She asked me where I had gone and I told her Santa Barbara, to get away from the fires."

Behind him, a small plane flew just above the skyscrapers.

"You can tell her my distress is because I do not perceive that she loves me. But she will not hear it. You can try. She does not know how to hear such a thing." He stood, and placed his hands on the window. "Long ago, you could open these windows, but then they realized it was too tempting for moments of despair. I would never jump out of the building, but I am still relieved that they took away the opening."

He turned to me. "Anna is my niece," he said.

"She's lovely."

"Do you love her?"

"I just met her," I said. "I'm more of a freewheeling type."

"Be kind to her," he said. "She is young. She doesn't know."

I took the bus back home, and the same group of men in

scrubs sat quietly, scrolling through their phone messages. The air-conditioning on the bus was loud and ineffective, but it was still cooler than standing in the debris of the fires, a fine sprinkling of ash over the whole city.

Where do people move to, after their houses have burned down? Many move to a new location, but some rebuild. They own the land, after all. They don't want to give up on the land.

I called the wife who said she would come in in person, and when she did I told her her husband was distressed because he was not sure if he loved her.

She listened, running her fingertips over her purse strap. "Interesting," she said. "Is that what he really said?"

"It is."

"And the wildfires?"

"Was a lie. He tried to let the cat run free."

"Huh. Didn't work, did it. Am I the cat?"

"I don't know," I said. "Are you?"

"Are you the cat?"

I shook my head, annoyed. I thought of calling Anna to meet up that night but she was too entwined with this family and I decided that promising as it was, as she was, I would have to let that possibility go.

"The cat is the cat," I said. "I will send you the bill."

"Charge me extra." She waved her hand in the air. "Don't be afraid."

"Okay. Thank you."

"In the Egyptian tombs," she said, vaping, "they buried trinkets with their loved ones as a way to express their appreciation."

I looked at her, unsure what she meant.

"So I will pay you as promised, but I also bought you this." She reached into her purse and removed a small velvet box. Inside was a pair of gold hoops, encrusted with what looked like diamonds.

"Oh, I can't—"

"I mean, you're not in a tomb." She pulled her purse strap back onto her shoulder. "But you're close, down here. It feels a little like death. Accept it as a trinket. Sell it. Get some extra cash. Please."

"I—"

"Take it," she said, hard.

"Thank you."

She stood at the door. Down the hall, one of the security guards put in a call for a pizza. The woman just stayed there, standing. It was like she couldn't quite leave, and for the first time since I'd met her, fear began to move beneath her features.

"You know," she said, "someone else has gone missing."

"You mean for a case?"

"It's me," she said, too brightly. "Me."

"You've gone missing? Aren't you right here?"

We held eyes for a moment, because the answer was so apparent. Since I'd met her, she had been nothing but absence embodied.

She rolled her back against the doorframe a little. "Can you find me?" she said.

She couldn't keep the flirtation out of her gesture. But the question was real. It was the realest thing she'd asked me by far.

I shook my head and then started to look in my files for numbers of others, psychiatrists, pastors, rabbis, therapists,

meditation classes, metaphysical counselors, existential phi-
losophers. But when I looked up, she was gone.

I went to sit in the apricot chair, still warm from her
ass. The afternoon was invisible to me, but I could feel it
out there, in the city at large. The weather and its aftermath
all happening somewhere above. And she was up there too,
dodging me now, making herself lost. It was a game. She had
bundled a real question with another question, and I could
likely find her body, yes. I could find her, even though that
was not what she was asking. A detective must have her limits. I leaned back in the chair and let her slip away.

Thief

by Steph Cha

After the funeral—lunch. It was customary, expected, a way for the mourners to come together on familiar, neutral ground, always the same Korean restaurant on Vermont. Jangmi didn't arrange it. That had fallen, like so much else, to her brother-in-law, her sister, the ones who could breathe long enough to make plans, phone calls. Jangmi could hardly speak. She said nothing at the funeral, only murmured and nodded as the mourners clasped her hands. There were so many of them. They crowded the chapel. It was the fullest she'd ever seen it, the pews swelling, the aisles crammed with wreaths. Isaac was only twenty-one.

They buried him, and she sat there, letting them do it. Her firstborn. Her one son.

She stared at her plate, piled with food from the buffet. Slick meat and boiled vegetables, greasy glass noodles. Someone had made her the plate and dropped it in front of her, nudging her to eat. She felt gas building in her stomach, closed her eyes and covered her mouth to swallow an acid belch.

The chair next to her squeaked as someone sat down. Jangmi willed herself to put her face together. No one wanted to see how she felt, not really. It would only make them uncomfortable. She sat up straight and opened her eyes. She'd never noticed the horror of this restaurant, the banquet rooms windowless, overbright.

Her niece was there, staring at her. "Auntie," she said, and pulled her chair closer.

Lynn's eyes were already red and teary, and just looking at her aunt seemed to make her cry harder. Jangmi knew what she was feeling—a deep but manageable grief, sharpened with pity. It was what Jangmi would feel if it had been anyone else who'd died. A church member, a friend. Even Lynn, her sister's child. Her face burned with the wicked thought—she loved Lynn, and she wouldn't wish this on her sister. But she would have traded anyone for Isaac, herself first of all.

She looked at her niece and felt a stab of guilt and tenderness. Lynn was twenty-three now, a young woman with a job, a boyfriend, straight teeth, and long eyelashes—fake, Jangmi realized, extensions put in at a salon. But Jangmi could still see the gangly bucktoothed girl, the oldest of the cousins by a short but important two years. For a sharp moment, it was all she could see—Lynn in a pink one-piece swimsuit, chanting, *Dig! Dig! Dig!* as Isaac and Christina plowed sand with their heels, building a Jacuzzi on the beach to Lynn's specifications. She wondered if that's how Lynn would remember him, as a sweet, plump child, guileless and laughing.

That child had been in him still, underneath it all. Among his tattoos, Jangmi's name on his chest, encircled in thorns and rose petals. The mortician had shown it to her, after he washed his body. A gentle offering, small proof that this boy, despite his sins, had loved his mother. She hadn't known it was there.

"Auntie," Lynn said again, her voice high and trembling, "do you have the money? Uncle Simon said to ask you."

Jangmi shook her head, still thinking of her name on Isaac's body, those ugly Gothic letters on his beautiful skin. The hole in his stomach, where the bullet had claimed him. "Money?"

"The envelopes," pressed Lynn. "The cash."

It took Jangmi another minute to catch up. The cash—of course there was cash. She had seen the envelopes at more than a dozen funerals, *geunjo* printed in formal Chinese characters, black on white paper. She'd filled them herself, with crisp, respectful bills, pressed them dolefully into the hands of bereaved relatives; she'd written her name in the books. It was part of the ritual, a way for friends and coworkers and church members to give shape to their regrets, as much a fixture as the wreaths, the Bible verses, the buffets. She'd forgotten about this detail. It wasn't hers to handle.

"I had them at the service, in that box. You know, that wooden box?" Lynn looked at her with desperate hope. "I thought I put it in my purse, but now I can't find it."

Jangmi shook her head. She hadn't even seen the box, not today. It felt wrong and dirty to think about money. What was it compared to the loss of her only son? But the fact was, they had budgeted that money. They'd had to purchase a grave, next to her parents'. Jangmi and Simon had saved for her parents' funerals; they hadn't planned for Isaac's. All these people—so many people showed up to say goodbye to the young. This meal alone would cost thousands of dollars.

Lynn lowered her head and cried. Not out of grief for Isaac, thought Jangmi, but fear and panic, for herself.

"Could someone have taken it?" Lynn asked. "Isaac's friends . . ."

Jangmi surveyed the banquet room, all the mourners talking quietly, hovering over their plates. There were so many people she didn't recognize, the young people especially. One of the pallbearers—his shirt untucked, his pants sagging—she didn't even know his name.

She hadn't spoken to her son in over a year.

She looked for the pallbearer and found him hunched over at a table across the room. He was with two other young men and one young woman. Even in their formal clothes, they looked like hooligans. One boy's head was shaved unevenly, like he'd done it himself without a mirror. The girl wore thick makeup and her tight blouse gapped between her breasts. Were these the people Isaac chose to associate with, over his own family? He had always bristled when Jangmi nagged him about his friends. But she had been right about them in the end, hadn't she?

Her heart quickened and the name came to her lips: "Teddy."

He'd been a pallbearer too—Jangmi would've protested if she'd had the strength, but he was the last person she wanted to think about while her son awaited his burial. She scanned the room for Teddy's skinny frame, the perpetual cowlick at the back of his head, where his hair coiled twice, like eyes. It was supposed to be lucky, and maybe it was: Teddy was still alive.

"Auntie? Did you say something?"

Jangmi shook her head. Now was not the time for a scene. She closed her eyes, hoping Lynn would leave her alone. There was no need to look anymore. She knew who had the money, and he was long gone.

Isaac died alone, but if Jangmi was right, Teddy would not

have been far away. He was never any good, that boy. She had feared him even when he was fourteen, smirking and smelling like cigarettes. His father, Chris Koh, was a notorious gambler. His mother, Mary Koh, worked two restaurant jobs, and worried after her husband. There was no time for her children, so they did what they wanted. The girl used to show up at church wearing scandalous miniskirts and colorful bras, the straps and hooks visible under her tank tops. Jangmi had seen her making eyes at the youth pastor one Sunday, her tongue sticking out between her teeth. She couldn't have been over fifteen. Teddy was worse. He drank and smoked and fought. But worst of all, he chained himself to Isaac.

She looked for him, after Lynn came to her, but it was just as she thought—he'd slipped out quietly, or he hadn't made it from the cemetery at all. By the time everyone else left, they all seemed to know the money was missing. She heard them whispering, speculating, but Jangmi didn't join them. She didn't want to talk to anyone, not until she knew what she would do, and she didn't want to spend another minute thinking of Teddy instead of Isaac. Lynn stayed behind after the mourners dispersed. She enlisted the restaurant staff, scoured the banquet hall, but the money was gone.

Simon was furious. He talked about calling the police—but what could they do? Jangmi let him rage and obsess. It was good for him, in a way. He was more animated than he'd been since the shooting; maybe since Isaac left home. And he required nothing of her, just a sounding board for his anger and suspicion. He railed against Isaac's ggangpae friends, but also muttered about church members, colleagues, anyone who might need money. He even wondered about his own cousin, a quiet, intelligent, moral man, whose wife had been diagnosed with stage three liver cancer. If Jangmi told him she thought it was Teddy, he would insist on tracking the boy down, having him arrested. And maybe that's what she wanted. But after all he had taken from her, she would be the one to reckon with Teddy.

For six days, she did nothing. On the seventh, she called Mary Koh. She hoped Mary would know how to find her son.

"I'm so sorry, Jangmi," said Mary.

Jangmi couldn't bring herself to thank her. How relieved she must be, that her own son had been spared. "I need to talk to Teddy," she said.

Mary was silent, and Jangmi thought she might hang up on her. "What's this about?" she asked at last. There was unease in her tone, but it was still gentle, polite, deferring to Jangmi's grief.

"Isaac," said Jangmi, letting her emotions leak into her voice. "Teddy was his best friend. I want to know how my son spent this last year."

"Teddy—"

"Do you know where he is?" Jangmi wondered where a young man might run with thousands of dollars in stolen cash.

"He's at home," said Mary.

Jangmi blinked. "Where does he live?"

"He's home," Mary repeated. "Staying with us. He's taking all of this very hard."

The Kohs lived in a two-bedroom apartment in Koreatown. Jangmi knew where it was, but had never been inside before. It looked small and messy—Mary Koh wasn't much of a housekeeper—not the kind of home that lent itself to entertaining. But Isaac had spent a lot of time here. The boys had been inseparable since high school, even after Jangmi banned Teddy from her house.

Mary motioned her inside. Teddy was nowhere in sight. "Come in," she said. "I'll make tea."

Jangmi stayed where she was and scanned the apartment openly. There were three doors that she could see, and all of them were closed. "Thank you, Mary. But I'd like to speak to Teddy."

"Of course. But here, let's sit down first." She went into the living room and waited for Jangmi to follow. "Tea will be ready in just a minute."

A door opened, and Mary's face tightened around her mouth.

Teddy shuffled down out of his room. He looked even thinner than usual in a limp undershirt and sweatpants. There were large flakes of dandruff in his hair. He bowed without looking her in the eye and mumbled, "Hi, Isaac-Umma."

"He's not feeling well," said Mary quickly. "Isaac, you—"

"It's okay, Umma," he said, interrupting her. Then he turned to Jangmi. "We can talk in my room."

She nodded and followed him without another word to Mary. He closed the door and offered her a seat on an enormous beanbag on the floor. He went to his bed, half sitting, half lying under the rumpled covers. The room smelled stale and musky.

He said nothing, waiting for her to speak. He still wouldn't look at her. He seemed ready to lie down and turn his face to the wall.

"I thought you'd be hiding," she said.

"I'm not."

"Did you take the money?"

He nodded, or at least his head fell toward his chest. It alarmed her, that he didn't bother denying it. She worried she had wandered into a trap, though she couldn't imagine what more he could steal from her.

"Where is it?"

"Gone."

"What do you mean, *gone?*"

"Isaac said he called you. Didn't he say?"

She felt the blood drain from her face. Isaac had called her. He left an incoherent message, begging for money. He sounded like he was on drugs.

She ignored him, and three days later he died. She didn't think anyone knew.

He sniffled. "We did something stupid, okay? And we owed someone a lot of money."

"Who?"

"You don't want to know," he said. "But someone scary."

She swallowed, trying to relocate the anger and fear beneath the swell of her guilt. "Is that who killed him?"

"No. But he would've killed him. He would've killed both of us."

Jangmi tried to organize her thoughts. Her son had died robbing a gas station, this stupid, desperate act the last thing he did with his time on earth. When the police talked to her, she didn't ask any questions. She didn't want to know the answers.

But now, with Teddy lying there, Jangmi wanted to know. "His car wasn't there, at the gas station," she said. "You drove, didn't you? And you left him there. To die."

His eyes went bright with tears. "I didn't want to go. I told him it was a bad idea, that we'd find another way. But he said we had no other choice. He said he'd go in, all I had to do was drive, and if anything happened, I should get out as fast as I could."

She wanted to slap him. Isaac was dead. He could never defend himself. And here was his best friend, telling his mother lies. Teddy was rotten. He came from a trashy family, and he corrupted Isaac, who was a good student, a good boy, before he met Teddy. It was Teddy who got Isaac into drugs and liquor, stealing and skipping school. It was Teddy's fault that Isaac joined a gang, that he never went to college.

"You took my son from me," she said.

"I didn't take Isaac from you!" he roared back. He let his head fall back against the wall and squeezed the bridge of his nose. "I'm sorry. I didn't mean to shout. I know you think that—you've never liked me, and I know you blame me for everything. But Isaac was an adult." He looked at her then, at last. "And you made mistakes too. You threw him out of the house when he wasn't the son you wanted. You never tried to understand him, or love him for who he was. I did. So you don't get to act like you're the only one in mourning."

Her face burned. He was wrong. No one loved Isaac like she did. Least of all this liar, this ggangpae, this thief. "You stole the money from his funeral," she said.

"I'm sorry. I had to. You can have me arrested if you want, but I didn't want to die." He had enough shame to look away.

"Where's the rest?"

"The rest?"

"The rest of the money. There must have been five thousand dollars in there."

"Six thousand." He let out a bitter laugh. "Sixty-four hundred. We owed ten grand."

"And now?"

"I owe thirty-six hundred. But I live another day."

She dug in her purse and found what she was looking for: her checkbook, a pen. This stinking apartment, this pathetic, hateful boy—how dare he lecture her about her own son. She stood up as she scribbled the check, tore it out, and held it to him. He took it, staring at the amount, and he started to cry.

"Thank you," he said. "Thank you."

She opened the door and Mary snapped to standing— she'd been waiting to see her out. Jangmi looked back at the sobbing boy and spoke loud enough for his mother to hear: "I wish with all my heart you had never been born."

Part III

manslaying

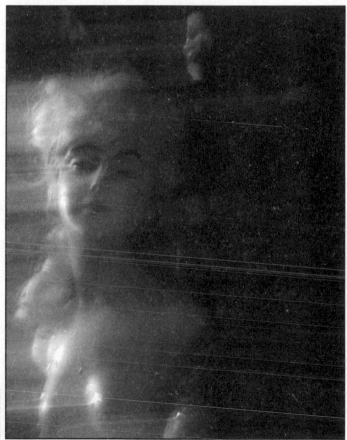

Laurel Hausler

Part III

Impala

by S.A. Solomon

For Joyce

It was raining, and the Impala handled sloppily. It steered like a cruise ship, but she knew what to do, because Glen, a former Navy pilot, had taught her how to drive and how to deal with sluggish controls. "Renée" (her mother, now gone, had given her the name), Glen would say, "you're in charge of the machine. If you fight it, the machine will respond, and that may be your last mission." Here he made his hand into a jet to simulate a nosedive. "Kaput, finis . . . splat." He always made her laugh, even when he made her angry, but until now, she had always listened to him.

He'd picked up the pieces after her mother left. Literally, since she—Renée—had smashed all the dishes and crockery in the kitchen of the government housing unit where they lived. She had no recall of this incident. Until he retired on disability, Glen had worked as a contractor for NASA in a classified capacity. She was too little to understand the whys of her mother's departure, but as she got older, various interested parties (usually female) seemed eager to offer her their versions. She didn't credit any of them. All she knew was that Glen took care of her, and in the times when he couldn't take care of himself, she did. She owed him that.

When the Impala began to wander, she gently tapped at the wheel and the car responded, straightening out on the rain-slicked, nearly empty highway. She glanced at the speedometer. She was within the posted limit. She was about to cross the state line and couldn't afford to be pulled over. It would be a "cluster-fuck," as the boys in her school liked to say. She hated that expression, evoking as it did (and as it was meant to) a female body pinned down by male members. The boys said it because of that, mouthed it meaningfully, hungrily.

If it was rape they meant, why not just say so? Cowards.

She knew what they meant because they'd shown her.

She was fifteen at the time and couldn't just pick up and leave, like her mother had. And she couldn't tell Glen, who would go gunning for them, or worse, report them and expose her to ridicule and shame with this public outing, a shame there was no coming back from.

She had a better solution.

There were plenty of guys in her school who wanted what she was prepared to offer, but only one who could give her what she needed in return. Protection.

Panda was a shot-caller. You didn't have to know anything about what he actually did to understand that. You could tell by the way the others acted around him. He was feared, and therefore respected.

So she was a gangster's girlfriend, so what?

At first it was thrilling, a dangerous rush. But then she began to crave and need the rush, couldn't detach herself, even when his affections, the butt slaps and possessive neck grabs, turned into blows and bruises she'd had to hide from Glen and her teachers. (Almost worse were the insults, the insinuation that she was "damaged goods" because of what those boys had done to her. She soon realized that Panda wasn't rescuing as much as recycling her. She would be expected to repay him in kind.)

Her teachers paid attention to her because, they said, she had "promise." Promise? What did that mean? She didn't owe them anything. She turned in her homework assignments on time and didn't routinely fail tests. That put her in the ninetieth percentile of her grade at the high school. It had nothing to do with the teachers or even Glen. It was because of her mother, who, when she thought Renée couldn't hear or understand, would ball up and hit herself with her own fists, would call herself *dumb, dumb, dumb*. And she wasn't. Her mother was smart, as smart as any man, Glen always said. But someone had taught her that she was stupid.

Glen wasn't like that. Glen had loved her mother. He'd met her at the blackjack table in the Seminole casino down in Hollywood. She nearly always won, had an affinity for the cards. It had gotten her banned from more than a few tables. Glen had tried to get her to teach him this skill, or trick, whatever it was, but she couldn't. Or wouldn't.

Renée had searched for the meaning of this. *Dumb* why? Was it because her mother had allowed herself to get pregnant and therefore trapped? (Renée didn't know who her father was. She'd never been told and didn't care enough to look for him once she was old enough.) Mama had finally freed herself, dropped Renée at a strange day care, where she wasn't even registered, leaving Glen's name and phone number pinned to her hoodie pocket. He'd gotten the call at work. That was when he still worked. She vaguely remembered the day care ladies cooing, not over her, though they acted like it. They weren't cooing before Glen, with his NASA ID badge clipped to his belt, drove up in the apple-red Impala, a 1976 Custom Coupe with a V-8 engine, a Turbo-Jet 454. He'd restored it himself. That's what he had designed at work: rocket engines. (Though she wasn't supposed to know that.)

She hadn't been asked to be born a girl. She would have preferred to be male. Not because she didn't feel "female." But because males were in charge. She couldn't stand the pervasive feeling of being controlled when a man entered a room with women in it. She didn't understand why she had to accept it, but as she grew up she understood that it was a kind of social compact. You might as well question the existence of God, or the weather. (She'd tried that too—not the weather, which was empirically provable, but "God." It hadn't gone over well in her conservative community on Florida's Space Coast.)

And Glen, who had taught her the tricks of machines and the laws of flight, couldn't counsel her on the laws of the girl body—how it would rage with passion and want, but suggest no acceptable outlet. Glen would not, could not, advise her against fighting the delicate instruments under her control. It was a confounding mystery to him, beyond logic or the rules of engineering.

He had taught Renée how to change a tire, which had started the trash fire she was running from. Well, not started. It had begun in school, when detectives wanted to talk to her about Panda's "gang ties." She'd been suspended for some doodling in her notebooks, which they'd seized from her locker (no doubt because of one of the helpful "tips" that students had been encouraged to submit through an "anonymous" hotline—a joke, because nobody was anonymous in their small town). The detectives said it looked like a gang symbol, and after all, she was the girlfriend of Panda, the "alleged" leader of the local clique of a notorious international criminal gang the authorities had a hard-on for.

They wanted to interview her, but she had nothing to say.

Panda wanted to talk to her too.

What "gang activity" had she observed? the detective assigned to the case (a woman who acted like she was on Renée's side) wanted to know.

What did they ask you? Panda would want to know.

She had observed nothing—only that, after word had gotten around that she was Panda's girl, the boys who had tormented her (the sons of NASA employees and of the families stationed at the nearby military base) left her alone.

She hadn't had to answer any questions yet, because the police needed Glen's permission. They hadn't contacted him, but it was only a matter of time.

Meanwhile, Panda had sent word around to find her. She couldn't stay home from school because Glen would notice. He was in a sober phase, having traded painkillers and booze for Jesus and taken up with a churchgoing lady. This lady acted like she wanted to mother Renée, but that was just for show, she knew. Anyway, she didn't need a mother. One had been enough.

Renée had realized it was time to go. Maybe that was what her mother had bequeathed her, an instinct for when it was time to take flight, while Glen had taught her the mechanics of it. She'd slipped the Impala's keys off the hook in the spotless kitchen (the churchgoing lady again). Glen kept the vehicle in the carport and never drove it now. He had so many DUIs it was safe to assume that he wouldn't be needing it in the near future. He sometimes let her drive, with him copiloting. They'd gas it up and go for soft serve at the Taystee Treat on the Cape.

He would probably miss her, but he had the comforts of the Lord and of the church lady. When that failed, the pills would be there, waiting.

(This hard-core version of Renée stepped in whenever she needed backup. But the hardness would melt away like runny ice cream when she started to feel the pain of abandoning Glen, who, for all his faults, had chosen to parent her when the ones whose job it was had run away from it. From her.)

She'd grabbed her gym bag with a change of clothes and the grocery money from its tin in the kitchen cabinet. It was her turn to go food shopping. Glen was big on discipline and chores when he was sober.

The Impala's powerful engine started up immediately and hummed, idling, as she adjusted the seat and checked the mirrors. She backed slowly into the cul-de-sac and shifted into drive, pulling out of the apartment complex and onto the nearby highway access road. She rolled down the windows, tuned the radio to the oldies rock station (another of Glen's influences), and headed north.

It was dusk on I-95 when it happened, a few hours later, in the green gloom of a conservation area somewhere past the urban sprawl of Jacksonville. The intermittent rain had stopped, but she had to watch for the branches littering the highway after a flash storm. And you never knew when the next band of showers was going to come through, decreasing visibility to next-to-nothing. Her hands felt slick on the wheel and she wiped them on her denim shorts. Her phone, sitting on the bench seat next to her, buzzed. Panda's photo flashed up on the screen. He had already texted her like twenty-five times and she hadn't answered.

The creature was fast. It raced across her field of vision and was gone, almost before she was aware of it. She stomped on the brake, the instinct all wrong. It was too late to avoid whatever it was she'd hit. The Impala fishtailed on the wet pavement. Glen's training kicked in and she turned into the skid, not fighting it as the big car slowed and slid toward the shoulder. The seat belt dug into her waist. She tapped the brake and straightened out, but something was wrong. The wheels were off-kilter, the car jolting as it rolled. She'd blown a tire.

She pulled completely off the highway into the break-down lane, as she'd been taught, and got out on the passenger side, away from the road. She'd missed landing in a drainage ditch by a few yards. She walked around the car to inspect the damage. The blowout was in the right rear tire. As she rounded the front of the Impala, she saw the point of impact. There was blood and gore on the left wheel well. It looked bad, like when the Kelly kid had tied a stray cat to his ATV and gunned it to see how long the animal took to die. He and his friends had timed it, taking bets. They were cops now, most of them. Glen had had his run-ins with that bunch. He didn't like their way of doing things.

The animal was nowhere to be seen—or heard. Either she'd killed it, which was likely, or it had crawled off to lick its wounds and die in peace. She mouthed a silent apology to it and returned to the rear of the car. There was a spare tire in the trunk. The only question was, could she remember how to change it? It had been a long time since Glen's lessons. She viewed the assembled tools—jack, lug wrench, wheel wedges—with some trepidation, and set to work. If she couldn't do the job, she would have to hitchhike, that was all. She'd hitched before. It was risky, but there were ways to protect yourself.

Truckers often had a soft spot for runaways; the big rigs that traveled with a relief driver, like a husband-and-wife team. It was, if not quite illegal, frowned upon for them to pick up riders, but sometimes they'd give a kid a break.

She had nearly finished loosening the lug nuts on the blown tire when a pair of headlights loomed in the dark. The last one was stubborn. She was sweating, her grip slipping on the wrench, and it jumped out of her hand. "Shit!" she muttered, searching the ground for it. She had a utility lantern and soon located it on the grassy strip. Glen prepared for everything, she thought with a pang, then hardened her heart. He probably hadn't even noticed she was gone, holy-rolling with church lady on the convertible couch. She wiped her hands on the rag and got back to work.

A few cars had passed without slowing, so she didn't worry until the vehicle's bright lights stopped behind her, the glare washing over the Impala and illuminating the trees with their glossy leaves. A drizzle had started up again. A man in a windbreaker got out. She couldn't see what make or color car it was, just that it didn't appear to be a marked highway patrol. That was good. She kept an eye on him as he approached but continued to coax the frozen metal part. She would probably need the can of WD-40.

"Hello, young lady. What seems to be the trouble?"

She looked up at a middle-aged man of medium build and average height, short dark hair, brown or hazel eyes (it was hard to tell in the glare) examining her in turn. Her hair was pulled back into a bedraggled ponytail and grease streaked her hands. She looked for the rag, but couldn't find it, so she wiped them on her shorts. His gaze followed.

"You're soaking wet," he said. "Why don't you give me

that"—he meant the wrench—"and I'll take care of it. A little thing like you driving this big car all by yourself? I'm surprised your mama and daddy let you out on a night like this. What is the world coming to?" He reached for the tool.

She shook her head and clutched it tightly. Her body was on high alert, the delicate instrument registering threat, and she shivered involuntarily.

"Take it easy, tiger. I'm just trying to help. You must be freezing. Here," he said, shrugging off his windbreaker and coming close, crowding her, "why don't you put this on?"

She backed away.

"Hey, come on now, I'm not going to hurt you. I'm in law enforcement—well, retired now, but . . . Look, here's proof." He reached for his wallet and flipped it open to reveal an official-looking silver badge, which proved nothing. He could've ordered it off the Internet.

"What's the matter, cat got your tongue?" he said. When she still didn't answer, his reassuring smile dropped away. "Do you understand English?" he demanded. He glanced around, looking for something—or someone. "Are you alone? Were you driving?" He grabbed her utility lamp and swung it toward the trees, as if to flush out a fugitive hiding in the underbrush. "I may have to call this in. Let me see your license. You'd better have one."

Actually, she didn't, just a learner's permit. "Keep away from me," she said.

"Don't be scared, girlie. I've got a daughter your age." Like that was supposed to reassure her. "What's your name? I should probably report this, but I'll tell you what. If you'll just calm down and let me help you out, we'll get this baby up and running and you'll be on your way."

Report what, to whom? That she was a girl alone on the side of the road with a disabled vehicle? That, apparently, was a crime. Or, maybe, not letting a man help you was the crime?

"Thanks, but I already called Triple A," she said. "They're on the way."

"A know-it-all, hey? You don't even have your hazard lights on, or a flare. It's dangerous on the highway at night. I can't be responsible for that, if something should happen to you."

Was that a threat or just the protestations of a man who believed, who'd been taught, that he had authority over "females"? He wasn't a first responder, someone with a duty to intervene (though what he'd be intervening in was still a question. This wasn't the scene of an accident—or a crime. Yet. And that *yet* nagged at her, woke the rage that flared when she felt—when she knew—that her "femaleness" was being turned against her and used as an instrument of terror).

But she couldn't scream or run. There was no one to hear, nowhere to run to. She could lock herself in the Impala and call 911. But again, how long would it take for someone to come? And wouldn't that just be the beginning of the end? They'd send her home and she'd be right back where she started.

She didn't know if the man was actually a threat, although her body was telling her that he was, that she should get away while she still could. After all, this was north Florida, notorious for its drifters and serial killers, who didn't look all that different from her pious, law-abiding neighbors.

Renée tightened her grip on the lug wrench.

The man watched her.

"Don't do anything you'll regret," he said, then laughed bitterly. "You know what? I've had it with you modern women.

You don't need men, is that it? You'll get along fine without us? Well, good on you. Listen, a real man doesn't want a girl like you either, trust me. You're better off with your own kind." He almost spat the last words but didn't elaborate. He didn't have to. She nearly smiled and bit her lip. The situation was far from funny. If anything, it was worse now, because she'd made him angry.

He turned away, as if to leave, and her brain told her, at this evidence of her eyes, *It's okay, it's over,* but her body, the delicate instrument, doubled down. Her arm swung up and over, the wrench connecting with his forehead as he spun around and lunged at her. She felt the tool hit bone; blood spurted from his split scalp. He reached out to grab at her, at the wrench, at consciousness, then went heavily down, rolling into the drainage ditch. Murky water from the rains lapped at the edge, closing over his body. She waited but he never surfaced.

She put him out of her mind as she finished changing the tire. It required all of her concentration: to safely jack up the heavy vehicle, swap the flat tire with the spare, thread the lug nuts, then lower it back to the ground to tighten them. She felt a sense of accomplishment as she did this. She returned the tools to the trunk and walked around the Impala one more time. Everything looked shipshape, as Glen would say—or as shipshape as it could get until it was checked out by a mechanic. That tire would have to be replaced, of course.

The breeze had picked up and she was sweaty and chilled. She took her hoodie out of the gym bag and put it on, shivering. She heard the lapping of water coming from the drainage ditch. How odd, she had almost forgotten about the man: her mind had closed over the violence to allow her to do what she needed to do to get moving. Now it washed back over her: fear, rage, a delayed sense of helplessness. But she wasn't helpless. She'd proven that.

She was frightened again, irrationally, since if the man were alive, he would have surfaced already. She heard a noise and gooseflesh prickled on her arms. She cocked her head, hearing the faint whoosh of faraway traffic and the evening trill of peepers in the swampy woods.

And something else, a faint whine coming from the direction of the trees.

The animal was mortally wounded. It was a wild cat of some sort, rare, perhaps—a Florida panther? As she approached, it hissed at her, even in its agony. She pulled off her hoodie and came close, speaking to it in a soothing voice. It quieted, probably to save its energy. Its life was draining away. The edge of the wheel well had caught and dragged the creature; breaking its back, maybe, since it quivered, its heart thrumming against her hands, but didn't struggle when she wrapped it in her jacket and took it to the car. In the light she saw that it had a tufted face. A bobcat, probably. Its fur was bloodstained. It was more dead than alive, but she couldn't leave it there.

That spark of life was precious, worth more than the predator's in the ditch. He'd gotten the burial he deserved. (Though she knew what the hypocrites back home would say: every life is precious in the eyes of our Lord. Every life like *theirs*, she thought. Men who were forgiven each time they strayed, abandoning their families, only to be taken back by the "females" who were expected to be meek and submissive and, above all, obedient. Females who were instructed to forgive the trespasses against them.)

She pulled back onto the highway, feeling the Impala drift to one side as it compensated for the spare tire. It felt like days had passed, yet it had only been a few hours. She would have to stop and sleep at some point, but not now. Not here.

She remembered how, one spring break, she and Glen had gone on a road trip and visited the Okefenokee Swamp. This was before his come-to-Jesus period, when he talked to her about science and empiricism, so she would have something to fight back with when the teachers at her school taught "intelligent design" as an alternative to the theory of evolution. This infuriated Glen: he would mock them, saying he had an alternative theory of flight for them to test: they should jump off a tall building and flap their arms, saying, *I believe I can fly*, three times, really fast.

Kaput, finis . . . splat.

In the swamp, they had learned about epiphytes, air plants whose seeds landed on tree branches and lived there, drawing sustenance from airborne nutrients and the shed foliage of their host. The cypress trees were ancient, centuries old, subsisting on the peaty soil. There were carnivorous plants too: flycatchers and sundews, which secreted a sweet liquid that attracted and trapped insects, then absorbed and digested them.

It was kind of like what had happened to Glen, Renée thought. Desperation made adults do strange things.

Bobcats lived in the swamp too, she knew, like the one breathing shallowly next to her on the cushioned seat.

She pressed the gas and the Impala sped across the Georgia state line, carrying them through the night and into the swamp where she would take the animal, returning it to the primal muck that had given it life, and was waiting to receive it.

Mothers, We Dream

by Cassandra Khaw

I t would, Henrik decided, always trouble him to hear his wife described as a barracuda, a sobriquet inflicted by her jutting underbite and cold acumen for economics, her predilection for late-year swims in the harbor when the water wore the ice like a wedding caul. Henrik loved her for those things. True, it had taken him time to acclimate to the uncommon construction of her mandible, even longer to adjust to the idea that she wasn't just *clever* but monstrously intelligent, frightening in her aptitude for retaining shipment calendars and accounting genealogies, the living cosmos of maritime trade in its storied fullness.

But that phase was inevitable in every matrimonial arrangement. Spouses, contrary to Grecian superstition, weren't born conjoined at the heart. Love mandated adaptation, a commitment to personal revision, no matter how hideous the reasons propelling that change.

"I'd appreciate if you not speak of my wife as such." Henrik spoke the words breezily, with enough humor that his peers wouldn't parse his remark as anger, but a dutiful concern for the conceits of decorum. He smiled over the brim of his tankard, the ale feeble, barely deserving of its title. In his pocket, the contract sat heavy.

Still, the room quieted and its drunks found reason to look elsewhere, their gossip turned again to how the king's warship had not only foundered, but failed to escape the inlet, capsizing before the applause eddied away. Thirty sailors died that bright morning and Henrik would have made thirty-one were it not for a miracle of abstruse circumstances.

"Come on, we wouldn't call her that if we didn't love her." Jamie was his best friend, unique among the immigrant Scotsmen in that he was both scholastically inclined and intrinsically tanned; a polyglot with ecclesial standards of discipline, prone toward melancholy but otherwise likable.

"Still," said Henrik, "I'd appreciate if you didn't."

Jamie shrugged, loose-shouldered. The tavern's population of regulars had been gouged by the recent debacle. Henrik, combing his gaze over the empty sprawl of tables, the faces of the barmaids creviced with boredom, doubted it would ever recover. Eight years ago, hundreds came, lured by the prestige of the town's pet project. Employers looked well on those who could advertise they'd labored for a king: monarchs tended to be lethally exacting on the subject of their whims, after all. Yet no one of efficient mind desired association with failure, least of all a catastrophe of such astronomic scale.

So they left. In twos, in fours, in families, belongings belted to their backs. There was no shame to the exodus. A mild embarrassment, perhaps, expressed in the hurried goodbyes and a reluctance to converse in absolutes. *We might come back*, they said. *Could come back, would come back, will come back, if the inquest ends in profit.* But no shame. The town hollowed of its borrowed citizenry and lapsed into a kind of half-hearted, shambolic alcoholism.

"I'd drink to that." Jamie emptied the dregs of his cider, the sunlight brindling his hair with bronze. It glowed on his mouth, his lips sticky with the gleam of the sky. "Tell me, Henrik, you ever plan to go back to your wife? The barracuda's worried sick about you."

He stiffened. "When I am better."

"If you can drink six pints of bad ale and eat a whole roast dinner by yourself, you're well enough to be a husband to the poor lass." Jamie palmed his cheek, chin propped on his hand, and sighed in bleary-eyed consternation. "Ingrid misses you."

Henrik gazed down at his hands—two fingers on the right still swaddled in bandages, a finger on the left shortened at the first knuckle—and clenched them both. When he spoke again, his voice was small. "I know. But we came to an agreement. It's better this way. I can send her money and she can keep the business running. I'm not in a position to be a good husband yet."

"And how will you ever get into that position again if you don't go home? Marriages can't heal from a distance. Are you scared of bringing trouble back to her? Is that it? Because I can tell you, it probably wasn't the Polish who sank the ship, if that's what you're thinking. And even if it were, they're hardly going to send assassins after a sailor and his wife."

"I hope you're right," Henrik lied. Outside, the day grew chandeliered with a salt-teethed murk, gray save for how the sunlight haloed the clouds. It bathed the skyline in a dreariness that seemed almost foreign after a summer of faultless blue sky. Unbidden, his thoughts gyred back to his wife's long white body pouring into the sea, her expression stern, even foreboding, as she sank from view.

In their time together, Henrik had only seen her smile once: an expression of radiant discovery and unassailable hope, tender in a fashion he had no idea she was capable of telegraphing, her face ordinarily so cragged with thought that Henrik had often wondered if that was why their life was barren of children, her body and her mind too preoccupied with her introspections to allow a baby into the equation.

But he had seen it. Once, precisely once. In the marine light of a sinking ship, skirts billowing from her taut frame, countenance ragged with worry until she beheld him in the gloom. She had smiled then and she had kissed him, exhaling air into his lungs, and to the end of his days he would recall that kiss, that taste of her, scalding and strange and sacred.

That sight of her, beautiful, exultant, bloody as a messiah, her mouth razored, her eyes utterly absent of light.

Ingrid sat in the atrium, stranded in the last light, a statuesque horror.

"What are you?"

There was an underwater quality to the scene, a sense of the world slowly distorting, swaying to the tempo of distant currents; a lack of static dimensionality, as though the universe might, at any second, cave into something more fantastical. Standing there, rooted in the vestibule of a home that no longer felt like his, an aurora of polished glass set in rosewood bruised black by the storm-tossed dusk, Henrik felt lost. Submerged again in the Baltic, swallowing salt water with every scream.

His wife raised her head, a discreet motion. Though her expression remained immobile, the needles in her hands continued to flash, the loop of feldspar-colored wool—a shade of flesh that brought to mind a memory of scalded skin—draped over her lap, expanding visibly between one breath and the next. Henrik had not known his wife to knit, but this came as no surprise to him. It was, as it stood, simply another aspect of her nature she had kept private, separate from their marriage.

Their eyes met and then her frown tensed. The door closed behind him.

Queensmen rode into the shipyard, flanked by wolves with doleful human faces, testaments to the wages of misdemeanor. Henrik glanced up as the men stabled their horses. Their uniforms were hornet colors, gorgets embossed with the symbol of the Crown: an antlered skull grinning balefully from the steel.

"Sweet as babes, the guilt-boys. Could pet them if you wanted." Jamie slouched an arm over the net-swaddled barrel and crossed himself with his spare hand. "Not that I would. They say they can smell the sin on a man from a thousand miles."

"They can bring as many guilt-boys as they want. They're not going to find anything here." Henrik mopped his brow. Even in the cooling year, the nights already annexing more than half the clock, dock work remained strenuous. It was not his vocation, however, and Henrik proved dismal at its execution, an ineptitude that alternately amused and aggravated the longshoremen.

One of the guilt-boys, its visage less lupine than the others, the brow more sophisticated, raised its head, turned as six women emerged from the nearby warehouse. Like Ingrid, they had the look of mariners, complexions weathered and warm-toned, arms cabled with muscle. Between each pair of them, they held troughs brimming with cast-offs from the day's catch: a stew of dying mackerel and withered shoggoths, the latter already calcifying into impotence, their pseudopods thickly rinded with salt.

"Be that as it may, they still need someone to hang. Otherwise, the gallow-birds will be callin' for the king's neck on the guillotine, and where's that going to leave the country?"

"In the competent arms of his queen, I guess."

Jamie laughed, the sound velvet and slightly mocking. He scratched at the bristling of white on his jaw, the hair on his head still resolutely black save for the silver flowering at his temples. "I heard he signed off on the ship's plans, which means he's complicit in those thirty deaths. *Thirty* deaths. You know what the barristers call that? Employer negligence. They need to do something. Otherwise, the country's image will suffer." He spat at Henrik's feet.

"I hope they leave the women alone, at least." Henrik thought of the flock of widows who had taken roost in the town, their relationships with each other familial in the wake of shared loss. Since the tragedy, they'd pared themselves of color and company that was not their own, spoke to no one save to facilitate their businesses, dressed in nothing but black like the throat of the sea.

And they made money.

Money as the town had never seen. Not even when the warship gestated in the naval yards, when merchants thronged the docks in hopes of sighting a monarch, organizing week-long markets; first for the bourgeoisie, then for anyone who strayed close to their vividly tinctured booths. The profits from that time were astounding, but a beggar's ransom compared to the revenue the women were now producing.

"Don't see why they wouldn't. Not when they've got better prey." Jamie palmed his neck and rolled his head back, wincing as cartilage crackled percussively. He slanted a thoughtful expression at his friend, mouth steepling. "You're going to be okay?"

"Unless they've given up on seeking out the guilty and plan on hanging the first fool that bores them, I'll be fine." Henrik watched as the women maneuvered their cargo to the guilt-boys, setting the troughs down in a half moon fencing the queensmen's mounts. He watched as the queensmen arrowed toward him, helmets sloughed, tucked under arms. At their head, a woman of tremendous beauty, tall and panther-like.

Henrik felt his breath sieve away, heard Jamie whistle a note of awe. If she had chosen the gentry, elected waltz instead of war, her likeness would have been sainted by the country's artists, the principal of a hundred serenades. Sculptors and painters would have martyred themselves on their mediums, hoping to possess her in their work: a look, a curve of the arm. Anything so long as they could claim it as theirs. Even now, Henrik wondered if there were poets haunted by her smile anyway, their dreams marred by her litheness and the ripple of her winter-white blond hair.

"Master Svensson? My name is Maja Torsdotter, constable in the service of Her Majesty, the Abbess of Wasps." Her voice was courteous, her elocution boreal.

He straightened under her appraisal. "I know who you are."

"My reputation precedes me, I see." Like her voice, Maja's smile was a wind-blasted thing, cold and sincere in its shining, fractured, glass-like brilliance. "That makes it easier. We require your assistance, Master Svensson. Follow us."

She broke his nose within the first hour, an act of mutilation remarkable for both its grace and the flippancy with which it was implemented. Maja evinced no enjoyment in the action, no rage, not even the immaculate blankness Henrik associated with psychopaths. If there was any emotion, it was fulfillment: satisfaction at a responsibility impeccably, if ruthlessly, performed. If there was any pride in this achievement, it was wholly clinical.

"You're lying, Master Svensson. Thirty men died when it should have been thirty-one. We examined the records. We *know* where you were quartered. *You should not be alive.*" She leaned forward, his blood still on her knuckles. "Tell me what happened that day, Master Svensson."

"It's like I *said.*" Henrik traced the rubble of his nose, felt the pebbling of broken bone beneath his skin. "I don't know."

"Do not play games with me." She crooked two fingers at the queensman standing guard at the door, a coltish-looking boy, taller even than Maja and Henrik both. He stared at Henrik, uncertain. Like Maja, his eyes were lacquered amber on ink, hornet hues throughout. "Bring the papers."

Her subordinate responded with a curt nod and retreated outside. He threw Henrik one final dubious look as he exited, his profile blue in the twilight, something like clemency in his regard, something like warning clenched in his jaw. The door shut behind him. The world became again Maja and only Maja, neither grimacing nor smiling, her gaze crystalline and steady, her brow faintly rucked, as though Henrik had given voice to an off-color joke.

"Master Svensson," she began again.

"You can keep saying my name as much as you like, but

it won't change the answers." Henrik dabbed at his nose with the edge of a sleeve. "I've said it once. I will say it again: I had nothing to do with the sinking."

"How did you survive?"

"Have you ever drowned, Miss Torsdotter?" The room held a single oil lamp, its glow staining shapes on the walls. Smoked fish—decapitated haddock, fat lengths of eel—dangled from the ceiling. "It is not easy. The body is nothing but instinct. It does not care that you're immersed in water, unable to pull air into your lungs. It will gasp anyway. It will kick as salt fills your throat. It will make you scream. So desperate to breathe, to survive to the next minute, that it will kill itself for that hope. And all the while it will flail, unsure why it is dying."

A wan breeze threaded itself through Maja's hair, the loose strands turned incandescent for a moment.

"Such trauma makes it difficult to remember anything, Miss Torsdotter."

"How did you survive?"

"I don't know."

"How did you survive?"

"I don't know." Henrik thought again of the water, of Ingrid writhing through the murk, of how much that sinuous grace had astonished him, her linens no more an impediment than the bloom of her long hair. And he thought of teeth, sturdy molars crunching through knuckle.

Mine, said a voice as his blood ribboned upward through the sea, as faces crowded his vision, as fingers pinched and measured the circumference of his torso. There'd been other voices too, babbling, a market's worth of fractious housewives conniving to bully discounts from the marketplace.

Mine! something screamed, and it had a face like his wife's, only longer, more silver, the prow of its piscine jaw giving off an unearthly glow.

Henrik shuddered.

"You shouldn't be alive, Master Svensson. According to the investigation, you were scheduled to be in the lowest stratum of the ship. Let's say that you, by some miracle, found a way to survive the initial clamor. You'd have still needed to traverse the rest of the ship. There wouldn't have been time, Master Svensson. The rate of its descent, the number of floors you'd have had to navigate in order to escape, the cold of the water—"

"You think someone helped me?"

Maja tipped her chin. "Yes."

"But that isn't possible, is it? You said so. The insides of the warship were a killing maze. Besides, what would be the point? What would I have to gain?"

"That is what I am trying to understand, Master Svensson." She opened her gloved hands, beseeching. "Help me. Please. This is bigger than us both. The Crown isn't without mercy. It needs answers more than it needs your life. Even if you had bargained with an enemy, it . . . I would speak on your behalf, Master Svensson. We just need to know what—"

"Would you believe me if I told you that my wife ate my fingers?" The words slid loose, fell wet and heavy into the silence, like offal into a waiting palm. "Because that is one version of the story I can tell. In this version, my wife is more than human and I've always known this. In this version, she swims into a sinking ship and she finds me, and she rescues me, and she takes a tithe of flesh because blood is the barter of the sea."

Henrik raised his hands, held them in the twitching yellow light. Thusly illuminated, it became possible to see how the scar tissue, whorled and still weeping pus, hid the scalloping of his flesh, the bones gnawed to stubs.

Maja studied him without comment, mouth pinched to a line, and then she sighed as the door swung open, her aide returning, scrolls piled in the crook of his arm. Behind him, one of the guilt-boys stood hunched, breath steaming between flat teeth.

"Guilty," it chuckled in an old man's tobacco-roughened voice.

"I would say that I believe you," Maja replied, her eyes on the guilt-boy. "But I would say as well that it does not matter. You are hiding something from me, Master Svensson, and I cannot forgive that."

She made a motion with a hand. Suddenly, the room reeked of musk, of hyacinth oils, of brine and meat still bloody, of salt, of heat rippling from the hide of a tortured thing, human skin on lupine bones; the guilt-boy grinned as it came inside, its eyes bleeding in threads.

"One last time, Master Svensson. How did you survive?"

"My wife saved me."

"Why did she save you?"

"Because she loves me." Henrik leaned away from the guilt-boy as it prowled nearer, its frame knocking against the corner of the table, nudging it back with a screech of timber.

"She saved you for love and only for love?" said Maja, voice soft.

"Yes."

"Guilty," chuckled the guilt-boy again, so close now, its eyes bright moons.

"I am sorry," said Maja.

Over the cliff of the guilt-boy's broad shoulder, he saw the queensman palm her mouth, despair in her expression, and Henrik thought, just for a moment, to say something to smooth it away.

"Genuinely, I had hoped it would not come to this."

"I understand," Henrik said, and shut his eyes.

The widows wore white when they came for him, silks dragging over the cobbled streets, the laces ribbed with dirt and soot. Ingrid alone wore black, her face without expression as she kneeled down, taking his jaw in her hands. Henrik reached out a hand, trembling, only to have Ingrid shake her head, an infinitesimal motion.

"You should rest."

"I told them nothing."

"We know," said the widows in chorus, their eyes black under the brims of their fascinators. For all the austerity of their attire, their millinery was extravagant: pearls and bone, coral cast in silver, gleaming fish scales, smalti and pebbles more vibrant than any gem Henrik had ever seen. He shivered under their scrutiny. "You are as worthy as she claimed."

It hurt. All of it. Where the guilt-boy had savaged him, where Maja had flayed the skin from his chest, pinned it to ribs with gleaming wasp stings. Ingrid trailed a hand down his sternum, her fingers rouged by their passage. The widows watched as Henrik pushed himself up on an elbow, back cold from whatever filth was trickling down the gutter.

"I'm done with this. If the queensmen find me again, I'm not going to survive another questioning. I can't help you." He spat teeth between each sentence.

This time, it was Ingrid who spoke: "Two more nurseries, you owe us."

"I don't owe you any—"

"Two more nurseries, two more shipwrecks," she said gently. "Otherwise, our marriage is forfeited and one of the others will take you for a husband, and you'll join your brothers at the bottom of the sea."

They had not been cruel. The widows, that night when Henrik Svensson thought to ask his wife *what* she was, had only walked him to the bottom of the sea. There, light pouring from their hair, they'd shown him what had become of the other sailors, the other husbands: their foreheads struck open, throats gouged out by their half-breed children, all eyes, all transparent radiance, their spines glowing gold.

"Please."

"Two more shipwrecks," said Ingrid, and she held him as he wept, the rain in tangles, heavy as hair, as kelp, as a ship drowned by a hundred pale, perfect hands.

Il Grifone

by Valerie Martin

At the rental car agency in Arrezo, to our surprise, we're upgraded to a Mini Cooper. This is a car we've wanted to try, and we head out to the autostrada in good spirits. The scenery unscrolls before us like a children's picture book, the colors saturated, the sky dotted with puffballs of clouds, the landscape an enchantment of terraced hills, vineyards, olive groves, and, perched high above in the bleached-out blue of the distance, the occasional hilltop town. We approach a bridge and say together as the slim strip of water comes into view, "The Arno." A few kilometers on we spot the hand-lettered sign for our friends' farm. *LA COLOMBA* it reads, above a painted red arrow pointing straight up.

Their driveway is a merciless, deeply rutted, rocky, steep incline that must be climbed in the lowest possible gear. The Mini takes it on without complaint. "I love this car," says Paul.

Up, up, and around a bend. The plaster walls and tile roof of the farmhouse come into view. They can see us now, or they can see the cloud of brown dust rising around us as we pitch from rut to rut, and they come out of the house to the terrace to wave encouragement. Sergio, the stolid Tuscan, and

Livia, his Roman consort. A last steep ascent and a sharp turn into the covered drive and we're there.

We rush to greet our friends with cries of "At last!" air-kisses, back-patting. It's been so long, too long, we all agree. They are well, or well enough; Sergio has back problems, and Livia is recovering from a bout of bronchitis. We're not much better, with Paul's arthritic knees and my bad wrists, but we don't much care, chalk it up to age. It could be so much worse. We proceed to the terrace, where Livia has set out plates of antipasti, bottles of mineral water, and their own red wine. The view is idyllic; the bright pots of geraniums, the vineyard, the cypress trees framing a scene of a tower shrouded in mist on a distant hill. We talk about everything at once: the children, all grown now, the weather, brief sighs about politics, theirs and ours, our journey so far, Sergio's recent trip to Tunisia. He's involved in a construction company of some kind there, though we've never been able to figure out exactly what it is that Sergio does. He's a big man in every way—shoulders, arms, hands, all muscled and powerful from the work he does in the fields. Even his feet are big. He gives the impression of always holding back a force field of energy that could wreck the world, yet he is, in fact, kindhearted and gentle. He talks to animals as if they are friends. He's telling us about an altercation they're having with a neighbor, a Romanian who is renting a small plot adjoining his vineyard and is possibly running some sort of illegal business out of his stone barn. As he speaks, Sergio's eyes skate past mine, once, then again, failing to engage. Or refusing to engage.

Something's wrong. I ask after their son Bernardo, an ambitious young man who is studying architecture in London, and Livia gives me a good report. Sergio looks at her, not at me. Paul is impressed; the school is famous and competitive. Sergio turns to Paul and tells an amusing anecdote about Bernardo's new passion for the pub crawl. I laugh with the others, leaning forward to take up my glass, purposefully putting myself in the line of Sergio's vision. He shows me his profile.

When we rise to transport our luggage to our room, Sergio walks with Paul ahead of me to the edge of the terrace. I follow with Livia, who gives me a hug as we part. "We are so hoppy you are here," she says in her careful English.

In the room, Paul drops his bag on the bed and goes to the open window. "Look at this view," he says. "It's like a painting."

"Why won't Sergio look at me?" I ask.

Paul turns to me. "What are you talking about?"

"He won't look at me. And when we hugged, he held me away a little."

"You're imagining things."

Paul always imagines I'm imagining things. He thinks that because I write murder mysteries, I'm unnaturally focused on the darkest possibilities of every situation. I'm always on the lookout for a sinister motive or plot point, and so I exaggerate perfectly innocent responses; I expect the worst, and I get it. But the truth is, Paul's completely insensitive to other people's body language; he doesn't realize he's irritating the life out of a waiter or a fellow diner until things get so bad that some overt hostility breaks out and then he's shocked. He's an affable sheepdog of a man, a bit bumbling, not slow-witted but not really paying attention, just wishing everyone well and hoping for the best. He and Sergio have been friends for thirty years, before I was even in the picture.

When Paul was studying art restoration in Rome, he rented a small apartment from Sergio and Livia. They struck up a friendship over their determination to speak each other's language. Paul's Italian is excellent; Sergio's English is adequate but suffers from desuetude. He looks forward to the practice a visit from his old friend affords.

So, it's not surprising that Paul didn't notice Sergio's reticence, but I know something's up. "I'm going to take a shower," I say to Paul, changing the subject. "You can go on over and I'll be along in half an hour."

Paul readily agrees to this plan, as it allows him some time to be alone with our friends speaking Italian. "I'll just wash up quickly," he says, heading for the bathroom. "Then I'll go."

After he leaves, I open my suitcase and take out a fresh blouse, my bath kit, and a pair of red sandals I bought in Milan. The shower is the usual drain in the tile with no curtain, so the entire floor is wet and slippery when I'm done. I'm thinking about Sergio. Is he consciously putting out a chill, or is he unaware of the change in his manner toward me? I feel dusty from the road and I wash carefully, drying myself with the nonabsorbent cotton towel, a puzzling feature of Italian life. I brush my teeth and apply fresh lipstick.

There is a small terrace, then a few steps down along the wall to the deep covered porch that shades the whole back wall of the farmhouse. I can hear Paul's steady Italian as I cross to the open double doors, and then the low murmur of Sergio's voice. As I step in, I can make out what he's saying. "It was on Via Silla, wasn't it?" he's asking Paul. "And the building had a name."

"Il Grifone," Paul says. I know what they're talking about

at once. Twenty years ago, Paul and I lived in Rome for a
year. After a long and fascinating search for an apartment,
we settled on a bright, airy flat in Prati, between the Vatican
and the Castel Sant'Angelo. The building, what Italians call a
condominio, was named Il Grifone because there was a plaster
relief of a griffin over the entry from the street.

Sergio switches to English for my benefit, but he doesn't
look at me. "That's right," he says. "Il Grifone."

Somewhere deep in my brain, my churning brain as Paul
calls it, a nerve end vibrates, a microscopic electric charge of
alarm.

"Last month I was in Rome," Sergio continues. "And at
a bar in Via Crescenzio, I run into an old school friend. He is
carabiniere now and Prati is his territory. I mentioned that I
had American friends who once had lived very nearby, nearly
twenty years ago. He was very interested in this fact. He ask
me your names and exactly where was the building. I wasn't
sure of the address, but I remember the cross streets. Then
he ask me if the building was called Il Grifone, and I say yes,
I thought it was."

"What did he say about it?"

"He said there was an explosion there," Sergio says. "An
old man on the roof blew himself up with the gas stove. He
must have left a burner on, and lighted a cigarette."

"Signor Batistella," Paul gasps, turning to me.

"How horrible," I say. "It must have happened after we
moved."

At last Sergio turns on me a long, searching look; a look
that says he knows I know what he's about to say. "It happened the day you left," he says. "Within the hour."

"How could your friend possibly know that?" I ask.

"There was an investigation," Sergio says. "My friend was on the team. The portiere remembered that the explosion happened just after the Americans left."

"And they concluded it was an accident," Paul says.

"They did."

"Think of that," Paul says to me. "Your old nemesis blew himself up."

"Well," I say, "I didn't like him. And he didn't like me. Everyone knew that."

"Yes," Sergio agrees. "That's what they told my friend."

"But we weren't there," says Paul.

"No," says Sergio, turning to me. "You weren't there."

Paul studies me as well. "It's like one of your stories," he observes.

At that moment Livia comes in from the kitchen, carrying a tray of chicken swimming in oil and garlic. We follow her out to the terrace.

"Are those yours?" Paul asks Sergio, referring to the chicken.

"They belong to the fox," Sergio responds. "But he shares a few with me."

Our Roman condominio, built at the end of the nineteenth century in what Italians call the Liberty style, comprised four stories of spacious, light-filled apartments, two per floor, high ceilings, tall shuttered windows down two sides, and marble floors that stayed cool all summer long and radiated heat in the winter. Our apartment occupied half of the third floor; our landlords lived above us on the fourth. The roof, a flat, white, heat-reflecting sheet of concrete where we tenants hung our clothes on cord lines that stretched from one side to the other, was accessible by a narrow stairway beyond the elevator. The clothes dried in record time.

On our first marveling entrance to the rooftop, we wandered around the edges, taking in the unobstructed views; we could see the Palazzo di Giustizia on one side, the dome of St. Peter's on the other, and when we looked down, the busy shopping street Cola di Rienzo, with its constant throng of pedestrians, motorini, cars, and buses rumbled exuberantly all the way to the Tiber.

It was February, and we congratulated ourselves on moving from the frigid misery of New England to the light bright chill of the Roman winter. We examined the clotheslines: a few sported softly flapping garments, linens hung wetly in abundance. "I guess you just use whatever one is free," I said to Paul.

"Notable absence of underwear," he replied.

We passed along the lines and came out into an open space. Before us, tucked into the northeast corner, a builder in a state of delirium had constructed a low-roofed, concrete, one-room hovel—perhaps originally it had only been meant for storage. Now it was clearly a rooftop apartment, capped with a brazen TV antenna. Two small, deep windows, barred like a prison, served to let in heat but no light.

"Does someone live here?" Paul said.

In answer, the faded green wooden door cracked and creaked open, and a gnarled, gnomish creature, dressed in sagging cotton pants and a heavy black sweater, confronted us. He carefully brought a lit cigarette to his thick purple lips and took a long drag, pouring smoke out through his nose.

"Buongiorno, signore," said Paul the affable American.

The creature made no reply. I noted that his eyes were

red-rimmed and his skin yellow, the pores enlarged from smoking. His grizzled hair was thick, curling over his forehead, and he had an impressive hooked nose that started high between his heavy black brows. As he brought the cigarette to his lips again, Paul rattled on in Italian—we're the new tenants on the third floor; we've just come up to see the terrazza, we're Americans.

Terrazza, I thought, was too elegant a word for the roof.

More snakes of smoke from the nose, as the man ignored Paul and turned to inspect me. I smiled politely. He stretched his chin toward me, as if to see me better. "Puttana," he said.

Whore. That much Italian I knew.

Paul took my arm gently and without speaking steered me toward the steps on the far side of the roof. I went along willingly enough, but I looked back to see the man watching me with an expression of such sinister calculation it made my heart stutter. In the safety of the stairwell, Paul said, "What a cretin! What is he doing there?"

"He's the griffin," I said.

Paul snorted. "He's got the beak, that's for sure."

And so we called Signor Battistella "Il Grifone," to the amusement of our landlord and the few friends we made in the building. Half eagle, half lion; on the ground, in the air, all predator, all the time. No one could remember how he came to be there. He was not a member of the condominio association, paid neither fees nor taxes as far as anyone knew. I was assured he was harmless, he was unemployed, possibly he received some sort of small pension, he was tolerated; he was allowed in that very odd way Italians have of allowing indigence and poverty in the midst of their affluence. When Paul complained that he had insulted me, our neighbors assured us that it wasn't personal. He was *maleducato*, a catch-all term that translates as *rude*.

I didn't encounter Signor Battistella again for several weeks, though once I saw him coming out of the market near the house with a net bag containing tomatoes and a carton of cigarettes. On another occasion, I glimpsed him entering the portone doors as I got into the narrow glassed-in elevator. I pressed the floor button with some urgency and was relieved to be lifted up and out of sight before he got to the stairwell. When I took the wash up to hang, I chose a line as far from his hovel as possible and pinned up my sheets and towels with my back to his door. But I always had a sense of his presence in the building, up there, mean-spirited, menacing. The look he'd given me as Paul led me away stayed with me. But I believed my neighbors; he was harmless, and I was the intruder, the outsider, the one who didn't get it. He was part of so much I didn't understand, a lot of it inexplicable hostility, sometimes alternating with exaggerated displays of kindness and sympathy. He was a piece of a complex puzzle I was gradually fitting together. That dark area at the top right-hand corner? The raptor eye of a mythical beast.

One gorgeous day in early spring, I went up just before dark to take down some linen I'd hung in the morning. Because the other lines had all been in use, I'd been forced to take the one closest to Il Grifone's creepy domain. To my surprise, when I emerged from the stairwell, I saw him stationed just beyond my laundry, peering down at the street. The cigarette glowed like a beacon in the crepuscular light, tracing an arc from his lips to the rail and back again. As I approached my clothesline, he turned and mumbled something I didn't understand. I replied with my usual apology for not speaking

Italian—*Mi dispiace, parlo italiano molto male.* He narrowed his eyes and took a step toward me, lowering his head and squaring his shoulders so that I had the impression he was going to charge at me. He wasn't a big man, but he was sturdily built, and as I dodged him, my heart racketing in my ears, I braced for the blow. He paused, holding out his cigarette between his forefinger and thumb, emitting a barking sound I took to be a laugh. Then he passed me and made his way—he had a lumbering gait, not a limp but imperfectly balanced—to the open door of his hovel. I could see past him to the fire burning on the stove; otherwise, the room was lightless. He went inside without looking back at me, leaving the door ajar. Hurriedly I pulled in my laundry, gathered up my basket and clothespins, and descended to our spacious apartment.

"Il Grifone was on the roof," I said to Paul as I came in. "He frightened me."

"What did he do?"

"Nothing really. He spoke to me but I didn't understand him. Then he laughed at me and went back to his horrid cave."

"Poor fellow," Paul said. "On such a night."

"It is a beautiful night," I agreed.

"Shall we walk to the Piazza del Popolo and have dinner at Da Cesare on the way home?"

"That would be perfect," I said.

I left the laundry in the basket and didn't get to it until the next day. It was mindless work, pulling out a sheet, folding it, stacking it in the linen closet, then pulling out another. I had cotton sheets and one set of expensive Italian linen that I had bought in an extravagant mood. It was always a pleasure to run my hands over the crisp linen from seam to seam, giving it a shake to flatten out the wrinkles. As I lifted the top sheet, something dark caught my eye. Was it a spot? Then I noticed another black patch near the center. I folded the sheet over my arm to examine the marks closely, though I knew at once what had caused them. Cigarette burns. Randomly spaced, five at the center, a few scattered on one edge. Neatly done; he had held the cigarette against the cloth until it burned all the way through, then moved on to the next.

My chest swelled with outrage, tears stung my eyes. I marched into Paul's study, where he was typing on the Olivetti he'd bought in Borgo Pio. I held the sheet before him. "Look what he's done," I said.

Paul raised his eyes over his glasses, turning to me slowly, not understanding at first what I was on about. I spread the sheet across my arms, and as I did, he saw a cluster of the burn marks and his eyebrows shot up in dismay. "What happened?"

"He burned my sheets!" I exclaimed.

"How do you know it was him?"

"Please," I said. "He was up there watching me when I went to get these. He laughed at me."

Puzzlement furrowed Paul's forehead. "Why would he do that?"

"Because he's mean. And he hates me."

"I don't understand," Paul said.

"Go up there and tell him we know he did it and he has to pay for my sheets!"

"Calm down," Paul said. "You know he has no money. And you can't prove he did it."

"Are you telling me you don't believe he did it?"

"No. I believe you."

"Well, what's to be done about it?"

What was to be done about it was basically nothing. Paul consulted with the landlord, who was as baffled as he was, and they agreed that a confrontation wouldn't be to anyone's benefit. Il Grifone would deny the charge. He was, the landlord explained, not entirely in his right mind, and it was best not to engage him in any sort of open quarrel, as there was no reasonable way to settle it. Perhaps, these two cowardly counselors concluded, it had been an accident and the remarks he had made to me, which I didn't understand, were by way of an apology.

"So I'm supposed to just throw my expensive sheets away and pretend nothing happened," I protested.

"Pietro thinks it won't happen again," Paul concluded.

"Oh, is that what Pietro thinks?" I stormed off to my desk.

I hatched a plan. I consulted my grammar book and made sure I had the simple phrase perfectly concise and correct. I used the familiar pronoun; there was nothing formal about my grievance. *So che l'hai fatto. I know you did it.* When Paul went out to the market, I took the sheet and two clothespins and quickly climbed the stairs to the roof. It was a chilly morning; the sky was overcast and the sun a thin patch of white on a canvas of smoky gray. I was pleased to find the door to Il Grifone's den open, and as I passed it, I saw him standing before his stove, cigarette in hand, his back to me. My knees were liquefying and I could hear my heart in my ears, but my mission was so clear and my sense of injustice so seriously aroused that I didn't falter. I hung the sheet on the line closest to his door, exposing the many black burn holes to the light. He heard me there, and turned to watch me, though he didn't approach; instead he crouched back, ready to spring.

I faced the door, with my ruined sheet flapping behind me. "Signore," I said clearly. "Signor Batistella."

At his name he leaped forward, just outside the door, barely a yard from where I stood. His eyes were black and dead, his mouth hung open, as if he were just waking from a slumber.

"So che l'hai fatto," I said clearly, indicating the sheet. "So che l'hai fatto."

He made a grunting sound, but I stood my ground. Then, opening his hands, palms out, and pulling the corners of his mouth down, he muttered the syllable "Buh." I recognized this time-honored gesture of indifference and dismissal. Paul translated it variously as "What can you do," "That's how it is," and "So what."

I backed away. My courage abandoned me. I walked briskly to the door and hurried down the steps. Letting myself into the apartment, I pressed my back to the door, hands on my knees, and for several moments stood there, taking long, slow, calming breaths. I was proud of myself, and confident that no one but my enemy and myself would ever know. Our enmity was declared.

I knew I was the innocent party, that I hadn't brought Il Grifone on myself, but I also knew that Paul thought it was like me to have found, so soon and so unequivocally, an enemy. I thought about, wrote about, entertained myself and my reading audience with the ways in which perfectly ordinary people can be moved to violence. Murder is my métier. Occasionally in interviews I've explained that for a writer like me, whose imagination naturally pursues the darkest options, my books are cautionary, because characters motivated by manic self-interest, by visions of revenge, or just by a fondness for mayhem, never think things through. I'm much less likely to commit a crime because I've thought about all the ways it can go wrong, and about how inevitably a clever detective is led to the devil by the details.

When next I ventured up to the roof, the sheet was gone. Perhaps Il Grifone used it himself, his animal hide indifferent to the burn holes. I confined my laundry to the far side, and was careful to stay out of the line of sight from his door. His message had been clear enough—he didn't want to see me— and I returned this sentiment.

Many months went by during which I gave no thought to Il Grifone, crouched up there by his stove. Our Roman life was full and busy. My confidence that a residence in the Eternal City would magically result in my speaking fluent Italian faded. I tried a tutor, a class, watched TV comedies, read children's books, but my progress was painfully slow. Crisp spring succumbed to sultry summer, and the sun beat down on my desk with such ferocity that it erased the occasional sentence I managed to inscribe on the page. I gave up long walks to the Orto Botanico in Trastevere and confined myself to short bursts to and from the nearest gelateria. Returning from one such excursion, my forehead oozing sweat beneath my straw hat, street grit irritating my toes inside my leather sandals, I waved to Edgardo, our portiere, always at his station observing the comings and goings of the residents, and crossed the few wide steps to the elevator doors. I could hear the old gears creaking as the car descended, according to the light button, from the fourth floor.

I heard a shout, followed by a stream of Italian. A high-pitched, girlish voice, raised in anger. It came from the car above, rapidly sliding into view. I discovered the occupants' feet first, the sandals and strong, shapely bare calves of a young girl, the worn black leather loafers and threadbare cuffs of a man, quickly revealed as Signor Batistella and a girl of perhaps twelve, whom I had seen a few times, usually in the company of her parents. They lived in the front apartment on the fourth floor. As the iron cage locked into place, the girl threw the door open and rushed past me, down the steps, and out into the street. Il Grifone lingered in the car, his head lowered, making a chortling sound and smacking his lips obscenely as he lifted his eyes to mine. I stepped back, gripped by a horror that rendered me speechless. He emerged from the car, dispersing a stench of unwashed flesh and cigarette smoke, and passed me without another glance. A word leaped to my lips, first in English, then in Italian. "Monster," I said softly. Then with vehemence, "Mostro!" He didn't pause. At the stairwell he turned toward the street and disappeared from my view.

I stood there, shaking with rage, my heart thudding in my ears, unable to move. I knew I wasn't getting into the elevator. After a few moments there was a ring from above, the long straps that hung limply in the dark funnel between the floors grew taut, and the car jerked and creaked as it began the ascent to accommodate another passenger. I backed away from the iron cage and dragged myself slowly up the three flights of wide marble steps that led to our apartment.

Paul was struggling with an ice tray at the sink in our narrow kitchen. I stood in the doorway, panting from the climb. "I'm making iced coffee," he said without turning to me. "Do you want some?"

"Something has to be done about that man. I caught him molesting a child in the elevator."

"Signor Batistella?" he said calmly.

"Who else?"

"I didn't think you would get into the elevator with him."

"I wasn't in it. I was in the lobby, and I heard the girl scream, and then she spoke very heatedly to him. When they got to the ground she ran away as fast as she could, and he stood there slobbering and chuckling. He was pleased with himself."

"So you didn't see what he did."

"I didn't need to see it. I saw the child. She's the girl who lives upstairs. She can't be but twelve or thirteen."

"Her name is Giulia. Her mother is a lawyer." Paul knew a lot about our neighbors in the building. He was on friendly terms with Edgardo, who kept him informed.

"I think we should call the police," I said.

"And tell them what?" Paul was pulling on his mantle of calming indifference, which always enraged me. "That you heard a teenager yelling in the elevator?"

"And tell them there's a pedophile living on the roof and that children are being molested in the elevator."

"If that were really the case, do you think no one would have noticed until now? He's been living there for years." In the next sentence, I knew, he would tell me how long we'd been living there. "And we've been here, what, barely eight months."

"We should at least tell the girl's mother."

"You mean *I* should tell the girl's mother."

"Well, I can't. You know that."

"If Giulia was angry, as you say, don't you think she would tell her mother?"

"We can't just do nothing," I protested. "This is a child, not a sheet!"

"Pat, be reasonable. I can't go up there and knock on the door and say, *My wife thinks your daughter may have been molested by the old guy on the roof. Just thought you'd like to know.*"

"I don't see why you can't."

"Because you didn't see anything. You're guessing. And you hate the guy."

Though it irked me, I did see his point. I had no proof. Just as I'd had no proof about the sheet, though it was obvious that Il Grifone was the culprit. Paul stood frowning at me, his mouth pressed into a thin line of resistance. It was one of those moments when I knew he didn't trust me because I made my living spinning plots. He thought my imagination affected my ability to distinguish reality from fantasy. "I am not making this up," I said firmly, and not for the first time.

Later that day, when Paul was out shopping, I went up to the roof to take down some laundry he'd hung in the morning. That was my excuse. I was possessed of a strong desire to see the monster in his lair. The sun was sliding down the hot blue wall of the sky, and the afternoon breeze the Romans call the *ponentino* ruffled my hair and cooled my cheeks. I went to the rail and looked out over the ancient city strewn serenely, forever crumbling, across its seven hills; it was a vista that never failed to ease and comfort my eyes. Then I turned my back to the low wall and faced the ugly front of my enemy's refuge.

The door stood open, and from my vantage I could see the hovel was empty. The ratty woven plastic lawn chair outside the door, a seat Il Grifone sometimes occupied, was folded flat on the concrete. I took a few steps until I was close enough to the doorway to see inside. The sun was at such an angle that it cast long stripes of light through the barred window and across the concrete floor. I took another step, then another, poised for flight. The door from the fourth floor was across the roof and it was sticky; I would hear it in plenty of time to race back to my clothesline without crossing his path.

The room was wider than it was deep, and there was a second barred window at the back, not visible from the roof. Beneath it, a narrow iron bedstead with a thin bare mattress was propped up by a brick under one leg so that it appeared to slump against the wall. A motley collection of plastic, paper bags, newspaper circulars, plastic containers, and a few socks was scattered across the mattress surface like continents on a map. At one end a saucer heaped with cigarette butts overflowed onto the floor. A metal table, laden with a few pots, dishes, an iron pan, more plastic containers, and two more saucers overcharged with cigarette butts, stood beneath the second window with another plastic lawn chair drawn up to it. The third wall was the kitchen: a sink on narrow iron legs, a half-sized rusty refrigerator with an early-model portable TV on top, and a two-burner gas stove, which, though small, was too big for the room. It was so narrow there was barely space to turn around in it. A closet, basically, I thought. Five steps in, five steps out. Not more than that in any direction.

Then I noticed something very odd: one of the burners on the stove was lit. The hellish little flame in that furnace of a room caused drops of moisture to gather over my brow. Why would he leave it on in this weather?

Before I had time to consider the possibilities raised by this question, I heard the crack of the roof terrace door. Without thinking, I darted across the concrete to my laundry, rustling in the thin breeze on the far side of the roof. I could see his pants legs and shoes as he passed along the side wall of his depressing domain. He didn't know I was there.

My last encounter with Il Grifone shook me to my core. It was fall, a radiant, crisp afternoon that provoked an astonishing and colorful bloom of cashmere scarves around the necks of Roman shoppers, men and women alike. I'd gone up to the roof to retrieve a few of Paul's sweaters I'd hung on the line; it was still warm enough for heavy cotton, and the marvel of clouds and sun layering streaks of orange, red, aquamarine, even thin lines of green and ochre, brought me through two long corridors of my neighbors' damp towels and sheets to the rail. I wanted to see if the sword held aloft by the angel on the Castel Sant'Angelo was touched with color, and indeed it was; it appeared to be glittering gold. Wonderful, I thought, turning to the other side to see the dome of St. Peter's.

Two lines over, there was Il Grifone, slumped in the lawn chair he'd drawn up to the wall, evidently to gaze at the beauty of the sunset. His face was turned toward the dome. That we shared an appreciation of the magical vista softened my heart toward him, but only momentarily. As I watched, he brought his eternally lit cigarette to his lips and slowly turned his cold eyes upon me. I was aware that his other hand was moving, turning over something in his lap, though he wasn't watching it. He was watching *me*. Smoke issued from his nose and mouth, drifting toward me on the light breeze. My brain was abuzz, taking in what I saw, weighing what I should say, should do, but I could neither move nor speak. He saw this, that I was frozen, and it pleased him. His mouth was slightly ajar and his tongue slipped out, gray and thick and dry. His eyes softened; he inclined his head toward me. "Signora," he said softly. "Signora."

Not *whore*, I thought. So, progress. Should I speak to him? His gaze rested on my face, a little dreamy, almost kindly. I could say, *It's a beautiful evening*, I thought. *Che bella serata*.

But I never said that. In the next moment his eyes, engaging mine, looked down at his lap, fairly bidding me to follow. His shabby pants were open, revealing his hand, which had never stopped moving, wrapped around the rigid and straining shaft of his penis. The tip, pink, slick, surprisingly healthy-looking, seemed to wink at me from its single eye. I took a step back and brought my hand to my mouth, desperately sucking in air to keep from falling down. He dropped his head back, and his eyes rolled up, losing their focus as he murmured, "Puttana, puttana."

I turned and stumbled past the ranks of towels and sheets, my hand still firmly clapped across my mouth, to the door. I yanked it open and staggered down the few steps to the landing. The elevator was coming up, doubtless the neighbors with the young daughter, my fellow in outrage. I didn't want to see them, so I took the stairs down one flight to our apartment. I realized I'd left my basket and Paul's sweaters on the roof, and I vowed I wouldn't be the one to retrieve them. I leaned hard on the doorbell, gratified by the grating shriek it made. I didn't let up until Paul opened the door.

We sit at the table, talking, drinking, eating, until the moon is high and the stars glitter overhead. At last, Livia and I get up to clear the dishes and Sergio brings out the grappa. They have a dishwasher now, an innovation since our last visit, and we make short work of the plates and bowls, chatting in the combination of English and Italian we've perfected over the years. On our return the men have lapsed into Italian and the grappa bottle has taken a severe hit. Paul looks up at me, his expression clouded, but not with alcohol; there's something chilly in his eyes, something I don't recognize. In the next moment Sergio makes a remark that amuses him; he laughs and they courteously switch to English.

I'm full and sleepy, but I sit for a few minutes while Sergio warns us not to be alarmed if we hear shots fired in the night—he's in a pitched battle with a boar that has run amok in his olive grove. Livia complains that she will have to cook *la bestia*, a process that takes several days. At length I excuse myself and, taking up the flashlight that hangs from the nail by the steps, make my way back to our apartment.

I've washed up, changed into my gown, and nearly finished unpacking my suitcase into the dresser when Paul comes in carrying a basket of bread, milk, and coffee for our breakfast. Without speaking, he sets it on the table near the window and puts the milk in the refrigerator.

"Livia looks tired," I say. "I think she's not recovered from the bronchitis."

He closes the door and gives me a look I can't read. "You left the scarf behind on purpose, didn't you?"

"What are you talking about?" I say. But dimly, I think I know.

"When we left Rome. We were in the car, ready to go, and you had to run back to the apartment because you'd left a scarf."

"What a memory you have."

"Sergio told me something else about what his friend said."

"About Il Grifone?" I busy myself folding a sweater and placing it carefully in the drawer.

"Edgardo saw you come in. He was near the elevator. He noticed that you took it to the fourth floor."

"For god's sake, that was twenty years ago. How could he remember that? I certainly don't."

"Obviously he remembered because he thought it was odd, because we lived on the third floor. And then he saw you come down the stairs very fast and run to the car. Signor Batistella came in from the market a few minutes later, took the elevator to his place, and blew himself up."

"And this proves . . ."

"Why did you go to the fourth floor, Pat?"

"Well, let's see. How about this: Pietro was my lover and I wanted to kiss him goodbye. Or maybe I pushed the wrong button on the elevator. Or we could try the truth, which is that I didn't go to the fourth floor. I went to our apartment, got the scarf, and came down the steps because someone else, not me, was in the elevator, going to the fourth floor to blow up the bastard on the roof."

"It's not a joke, Pat," Paul says coldly. "You had the time, and you had the motive. You hated that man."

"Not without cause," I retort. "But that doesn't make me a murderer."

Paul raises his eyes to mine, and I see they are wet with tears.

"Oh for god's sake," I say. "You believe it."

"I don't know what I believe. I wish Sergio had never told me."

And then I understand what has happened. Though I haven't changed, Paul will never see me in the same way again. This tiny poisoned seed Sergio has planted will grow into a towering evergreen of suspicion. Nothing I can say will do anything but increase Paul's distrust. Our lives will now be played out in the shadow of Il Grifone. I picture him, the shambling demon at the top of the building, stirring his bubbling, poisonous brew over a gas stove in a kitchen hotter than Dante's inferno. Tears press and flood my eyes. "I'm not a murderer," I say.

Paul, seeing my distress, relents, opens his arms, and wraps me in an embrace of exhausted kindness.

"I'm not a murderer," I repeat, sobbing into his shirt. He holds me fast, nuzzling his lips against my neck. But he doesn't say he believes me.

A shot rings out from the olive grove. Then another.

It was a cashmere scarf I'd bought on a visit to Lucca, a beautiful thing: soft, wide, and double-ply; dark purple on one side, lavender on the other. I'd left it on the coat tree in the foyer when I put my coat on to go down to the car with another suitcase. As we were illegally parked, Paul went up to get the last one while I waited on the street. When he reappeared, Edgardo came out of his room to meet him, and they said their farewells in the lobby. I stood looking down the street, and I spotted Il Grifone, or rather the back of Il Grifone, turning at the corner. Off to get his cigarettes, I thought. That's when I remembered my scarf. As Paul came out of the portone, I passed him saying, "I left my scarf." I greeted Edgardo on the landing and let myself into the elevator, where I pressed the button for the fourth floor. I watched the floors go by, no one was around, and then I pulled open the cage, crossed to the door, and went up the narrow staircase for the last time.

It was bitter cold with a mild breeze. The lines were all bare; it had rained in the morning. I stepped onto the concrete terrace and the sun peeked out to greet me. I went directly to the door of Il Grifone's miserable room, which stood, as in a fairy tale, wide open. Inside I could see the fire flickering on the stove, the only light in the gloom. It occurred to me that a breath of wind could easily blow it out. Really, he took quite a risk, leaving it lit, evidently, all the time. Was it to light his cigarettes?

A breath could blow it out, I thought. Not even a gloved hand needed to turn the dial. Just a breath. I looked around at the bare, empty terrace. All I could see from this vantage was the brightening sky, the clouds clearing off fast. I focused again on the little flame. Just a breath, I thought. Five steps in. And five steps out.

Miss Martin

by Sheila Kohler

I

When Diane comes back from boarding school this summer, she finds her father waiting in the still afternoon air. Diane usually walks to their quiet town house on a shady side lane in East Hampton, but today her father lounges in his tight blue jeans and his Panama hat in the shade of a tree at the bottom of the station's steps.

"Oh, there you are, Kitten," he says, his narrow face brightening, as she descends from the platform, dragging her fancy suitcase behind her. Diane's father calls her *Kitten* or sometimes *Pussy Cat* because of her soft dark eyes, he says. He keeps, she knows, a photo of her as a little girl with blond curls and a bow in her hair on his desk in his office in an oval silver frame.

Diane is aware her father is considered a distinguished-looking man, with his fine profile, the delicate pointed nose, though he has lost much of his hair. He wears the Panama hat all through the summer to protect and hide his bald pate. Tall and slender, he moves quickly to take her suitcase from her and to kiss her hard on both her cheeks. "I'm so glad you are home," he says, looking into her eyes.

She says politely, "Thanks for coming to get me," as he swings her suitcase into the trunk of his old gray Mercedes, though she worries immediately that he is here in order to reprimand her in the privacy of his car. She is afraid her headmistress, Miss Nieven, might have phoned him from the school as she had threatened to do. What if they have decided to expel her?

Her father, a lawyer, has very strict ideas of what is right and wrong and often holds forth at length about the evils in the world: dishonest politicians, corruption in the government, and unfaithful wives, always sounding shocked and angry.

But when she gets into the familiar car and her father starts the engine, he says nothing about school. Instead, he turns to her and confides apologetically that the work which was supposed to be done on their house has not been completed.

"They told me they would have it finished weeks ago, but of course they are still working on it," her father warns, speaking of the new sleeping loft he has installed on one side of the house. "They haven't put in the stairs yet," he adds, and glances at her anxiously with his close-set, intensely blue eyes.

"Does she like it?" Diane asks, referring to her father's second wife. It is the first time Diane has been in the house without her mother and with Miss Martin—Diane always thinks of her as Miss Martin—who was her father's secretary and is now his wife.

He glances at her with something close to impatience and purses his thin lips as though her question is extraneous. "No, she calls it the slave quarters," he says with sarcasm and scowls, driving skillfully down Town Lane, threading in and out of the cars, pale clouds vanishing across the sky.

Diane just looks at him and wonders why he has bothered to go to the expense of altering the house now that her mother has gone. She thinks of her maternal Kentucky grandmother saying, "Closing the barn door when the horse has bolted."

Could it be simply out of spite?

Diane's father is from an old New England family where thrift is prized and ostentatious wealth frowned upon. She knows her father does not like unnecessary expense. Though he is more than generous with her at times, he is basically a thrifty man who despite his excellent salary in the law firm and his inheritance never takes a taxi and says disparagingly that first class on an airplane is "for people with fat behinds." Diane's father does not have a fat behind, she knows. He keeps himself trim by running for an hour at six every morning and eating little.

The sleeping loft was something her mother wanted to have built. She always found the two-bedroom house too small, too cramped, claustrophobic. "It's like a boat!" she would say in exasperation—Diane can hear the way her mother says *boat* with such disgust, as if she were naming something much more damning and using some other unmentionable word.

When her father shuts the car's engine off in the driveway of the white clapboard house, he glances at the small red Renault parked there and whispers, "Things are rather disorganized at home, I warn you. We will have to be patient, Kitten."

She sits beside him uncomfortably in the shade of the magnolia tree, looking up at the house with some apprehension.

She stares at the creeper-covered dormer window of her small bedroom and thinks of her large, sunny dormitory at school which she shares with two other girls and where she makes her narrow bed so neatly, with hospital corners, pulling the bright plaid blanket tightly across the top. She keeps her one small bookcase close by her bedside with her favorite books which she has organized since she was quite small in alphabetical order. She thinks of her history teacher who has given her an A+ for her paper on regicide—she wrote about Charles I, Louis XVI, and Nicolas II of Russia. Mrs. Kelly had read the paper to the class as an example of excellent work. "Listen to the scope of this paper!" she had said, while Diane sat feeling her face turn crimson. What will Mrs. Kelly say now if she hears about what Diane has done? What if she can never return to her history class?

Diane stares at the creeper-covered house, with its small dormer windows, where she has lived all her life, as though she has never seen it before, hesitating to enter until her father says, "Come along, Kitten. Got to face the music," and they enter the living room together, her father carrying her suitcase.

II

The first thing Diane does in the house is climb up the long ladder which is propped against the wall of the dining room going into the high loft which runs all the way above the kitchen and dining room.

"Wow!" she says when she gets to the top, standing in the part of the loft where the sloping roof is highest. "You could sleep seven up here." She peers at the expanse of the long, low room and then down from the open door to her father who stands watching her from below.

She thinks of her mother who always said the space

above the kitchen and the dining room was wasted. She had said in what, Diane understood, was an effort to persuade her father, that this way Diane could have lots of friends over if she wanted to in the summers when everyone liked to come to a house near the sea. It would be good for her. Diane, despite her house near the sea, has never had lots of friends who want to come over. She is too quiet, too shy, too bookish, to have made many friends. She is not one of the popular pupils at school. She likes spending her holidays alone in the small, shaded back garden with its white roses which her mother grew in shiny blue pots, just reading or swimming in the sea.

Sometimes Diane thought her mother wanted to put *her* in the sleeping loft on the other side of the house, so that her mother could have a room of her own where she could work on her books, or even just sleep on her own if she was so inclined. Diane had often found her father on the leather sofa in the living room when she came down in the morning for her breakfast. He would watch her coming down the stairs and sigh sadly, shrugging his shoulders as if to say: *You see how your mother treats me.*

"Come down now and say hallo," her father calls up to Diane. "Be careful, Kitten, come down backward," her father says, holding the long ladder as Diane descends fast into the small dining room which opens onto the living room.

She expects Miss Martin to come forth from the kitchen in her narrow dark skirt with the small slit up the back, with a cup of delicious frothy coffee in her hands, as she would as her father's secretary.

But to Diane's surprise Miss Martin is not in the kitchen whipping up a soufflé and must be upstairs in one of the bedrooms. She soon comes wafting down the stairs and into the cramped living room with its overflow of Victorian furniture, the pink chintz-covered chairs, the leather sofa, and the large fireplace. She looks too tall for the low-ceilinged room and she is smiling in a silly way.

Miss Martin, Diane will later learn when she goes to study abroad in France, is what the French call a pretty/ugly woman. She has a strong profile, a large nose, plump lips, and high cheekbones. Her glossy dark hair, which in the office was expertly coiled at the back of her head, is now springing rebelliously around her face despite the strange sort of *Alice in Wonderland* ribbon which circles her head, as though she were a child. Her makeup, Diane notices, has changed. Though Diane does not yet wear any, as her father prefers she does not, she has been studying the question. In the office Diane noted Miss Martin's makeup was impeccable: the lipstick discreetly pink, the mascara a faint blue echoing the color of her pale eyes, the foundation cream perfectly smooth and light. Now it has become suddenly violent: she has glossy red lips and dark mascara and dark foundation cream.

She is not in her skirt but instead a long loose dress with lots of bright red flowers which Diane feels does not suit her at all. She seems to be wearing strong perfume.

She does not shake Diane's hand firmly as she would do in the office, but lurches forward and seems almost to fall on Diane. She enfolds her in a huge hug, hanging onto her as though she cannot stand on her own. She gives her a damp kiss, which Diane is tempted to wipe from her cheek. Why is she kissing her! Diane hates physical contact with strangers. Miss Martin gushes, "Goodness, how you have grown up! A young lady! I love your hair like that!" Diane has cropped her fair hair short like a boy. She just looks at Miss Martin, aghast.

There is a moment of awkward silence. Then Miss Martin laughs in a girlish way and says they are both just to relax; she will bring in lunch in a jiffy. Diane is hungry, not having had time for breakfast before she took the early train, and she imagines that Miss Martin, despite her strange attire, will make something splendid for this first luncheon together.

III

Diane first heard about Miss Martin before she met her. Miss Martin was, Diane's father said, smiling in a satisfied way, "the perfect secretary, remembers everything, but is utterly discreet, always there when you need her; never there when you don't."

Miss Martin moved around her father's office in her perfectly pressed long-sleeved blouse, the smooth sheer stockings on her long legs whispering seductively as she walked. The first time Diane saw her she wanted to touch the stockings and perhaps even the slim legs which seemed to go on forever.

Diane was immediately fascinated by Miss Martin's obvious efficiency, the neatness of her desk, and her very high-heeled patent-leather shoes which rapped out commandingly on the parquet floor. She was fascinated by the way she moved so fast around Diane's father, the way she answered the telephone so swiftly as though plucking up a weed from the garden, and the clipped way she pronounced the names of her father's law firm. Diane presumed Miss Martin was English until her father said she came from South Africa. "Albee, Melbourne, and Morton," she said commandingly, as though announcing the regiments in an army. Diane's father is the *Morton* part.

"Why did they put your name last?" Diane once asked her father.

"Alphabetical order," her father replied quickly. Diane wonders if that was true.

IV

Diane and her father sit opposite one another in the pink armchairs in the dark living room beside the empty fireplace in the steamy summer air. There is no air-conditioning in the house—"waste of energy," her father says. Faintly in the distance they can hear the sound of waves. The house is not far from the shore. Diane's father loves the sea and still likes to take his daughter there sometimes at twilight in his car.

"How's school? Did you miss me?" he asks.

There is not much Diane can say under the circumstances, and her father hardly seems to be listening anyway. "Fine. I got all As." She glances around the room. She has never had problems at her school before this. She loves her classes, most of her teachers, and has always had the best marks in the class.

There is a moment of silence, and Diane notices that the photo of her and her mother which always stood on the top of the old English dresser is gone. "The photo!" she says to her father, who shrugs and looks a little embarrassed.

"We put it upstairs in your room, Kitten."

Diane is about to say something rude but decides it would be better not to considering her situation.

It was her mother who with considerable difficulty had persuaded her father to send Diane to a select girls' boarding school in Connecticut which costs, as her father says, "a fortune."

"It would actually save you money, as she would not be around for you to spoil rotten," her mother had said, staring severely at him. Despite his thrifty upbringing, her father would from time to time buy Diane expensive gifts from the fancy shops in East Hampton: soft cashmere sweaters in pastel colors, gold bracelets, once a charm bracelet with a heart.

Her father had protested, sulked, asked her if she no longer loved him, insisted the school catered only to snobs, the rich and the privileged, and he had finally driven her there in silence the entire way when she went off for the first time at thirteen. He had lingered on in the long driveway when all the other parents had left. She had watched him from the dormitory window sitting there in his car, the sun sinking between the old oaks at the end of the driveway, his shoulders shaking. She hoped no one else had seen her father weep.

She is expected to contribute to her exorbitant school fees, in any way she can. ("At least you could make an effort to help me," her father had said.) When she turned sixteen this year, she was allowed to work in the mailroom, sorting the mail at the school for a small hourly wage. "It's not much money," Diane told her father apologetically. He just smiled and said he was proud of her and kissed her hard. He said it was not the money but the willingness to work that was important in life. Diane's father admires people who work hard, whatever they do, or so he says. He says that the less one is paid, the more meaningful the work often is, though he is very well paid himself as a lawyer, though she knows he does do pro bono work occasionally.

Diane imagines he admired Miss Martin because she was so good at her work as a secretary, taking down his every word so exactly, and dealing with the complexities of the computer so efficiently, something he has never learned to do, all for a small salary. He must have thought she would make a good, hardworking wife.

They sit opposite one another in silence listening at the same time to certain ominous noises coming from the kitchen.

"So, nothing to report?" Diane's father asks.

She shrugs and shakes her head.

Her father seems not to have heard about the missing letters and packages in the mailroom (sometimes there was cash in the envelopes, sometimes delicious cookies in the packets). The headmistress, Miss Nieven, has apparently not called as she had threatened, to discuss the matter. "I will have to decide with your parents what to do about this, Diane," Miss Nieven had said ominously in the seclusion of her dark, book-lined study. "Quite frankly, I don't really understand your behavior. You come from an affluent family after all, your father a lawyer, your mother a full professor, a house in East Hampton. You are always beautifully dressed. I know you have had difficult changes in your life to cope with recently, but you have everything you need, surely?" Miss Nieven had said, staring at her. "You realize this is a serious matter. How would you like it if your father had sent you a package and you never received it?"

"My father has never sent me a package or even a letter," Diane had replied. Her father only gives her presents in person. She looked at Miss Nieven and thought that now perhaps as her mother was in France where she had gone off with her lover, a French professor she met at the university where she teaches philosophy in Southhampton, she might send her packages. She hopes her mother will send her some French books. She is learning to speak French at school. She would like to speak a language which is not her mother tongue.

At this point they are distracted by a great clatter of dishes and pots and pans and the strong odor of something burning.

"Perhaps you better go and see if you can help, Kitten," her father suggests.

Miss Martin is standing in the middle of the big, hot kitchen with its glass-fronted cabinets and old wooden table with several pots bubbling furiously on the stove, a frying pan smoking, and a serving platter—Diane sees it is the good blue-and-white Wedgewood one, which her father inherited from his Connecticut grandmother, which has broken at her feet. She is, to Diane's consternation, weeping.

"Can I help?" Diane says as her father comes striding into the kitchen. He turns off the gas under the smoking pan and the bubbling pots and takes out a broom from the closet. He vigorously sweeps up the broken crockery from the floor into a dust pan and throws the pieces into the rubbish bin. Diane and Miss Martin stand and watch. He says severely, "I will get some sandwiches," and Miss Martin weeps even louder, as he walks out of the house, slamming the door behind him.

V

At night in her bedroom Diane lies awake reading. It rained earlier that evening and with her window open, she can hear the sound of the waves in the distance and smell the fresh odors of the garden mixed with something dead. In the faint light of the bedside lamp, she looks at the photo of herself and her mother on the dresser and the small silver pitcher of white roses which someone has arranged beside it. Could it have been Miss Martin? From the bedroom next door Diane hears her father's loud voice and Miss Martin's cries. She hears her wail, "What do you want me to do?"

In the morning at breakfast when Diane goes down into the kitchen her father has bought a coffee cake and makes the coffee and even squeezes the oranges for juice himself (he likes his orange juice fresh squeezed). Miss Martin sits red-eyed at the kitchen table in her dressing gown, her hair in disarray, staring blankly before her, her big hands folded in her lap, as though she were an unhappy guest.

Then Diane's father says he has work to do, but will be back and would like his lunch promptly at one, if that is not too much to ask. He leaves them sitting side by side in silence at the wooden table where Diane's mother would chop vegetables and make her delicious soup.

When the door shuts on her father, Miss Martin starts weeping again, and Diane wants to give her a shake. What is wrong with the woman? She does not seem able even to clear the kitchen table of the breakfast dishes or the orange peels, which Diane does, stacking the dishes in the dishwasher with a clatter. Obviously Miss Martin is not used to kitchens but offices.

Miss Martin looks up at Diane and says, "A mistake. A terrible mistake! I thought it would be so different! He seemed such a good man, such a devoted father!"

Diane thinks about this and is not sure what to say in response, though she would like to agree. Then she says, "What can I do?"

Miss Martin looks at her, apparently thinking about the matter. "I just wish I could escape—marriage is so different from work where you get to escape at least in the evenings and on the weekends to gather your wits. This just goes on and on!"

Diane laughs and says that is true. "I know just what you mean about wanting to escape."

"You do?" Miss Martin says.

Diane thinks of how often she had wished to escape before she finally managed to persuade her mother to send her to boarding school when she turned thirteen.

Once she had tried to tell her mother about her father and what he would do in the car at the beach in the gloaming. She must have been nine or ten, but her mother had interrupted her in the midst. When she said something about her father's hand and where it went, her mother had looked uncomfortable and sighed. She said, "Pet, all little girls make up stories in their minds about their fathers. It's difficult to sort out what is real from fantasy in life. I remember doing that myself as a child. One day you will read Freud and understand why."

Diane could think of nothing to say to that at the time. Now she tells Miss Martin, "Yes, I wanted so badly to leave home. Sometimes I thought of running away."

"To get away from your father?" Miss Martin says, and looks at Diane and seems to understand.

She nods and says, "I tried to tell my mother, but she didn't understand."

What Diane wanted to tell her mother was that she would never make up a story like this: this was real, her father driving her to the beach at twilight, leaving the car motor running and staring as if mesmerized at the sea, murmuring to her on and on like the waves beating against the shore about things she would have preferred not to hear. He would sigh and breath in an odd loud way, his hand straying so strangely and surprisingly. Each time, though she feared it was coming, it was a shock, the long fingers slithering from his knee across to hers and finding their way like a snake between her legs, stroking her like a kitten, almost as if the hand had nothing to do with her father.

Yet he would eventually say, "You like that, don't you?" and she, weeping, would shake her head.

"Please don't," she would beg him.

"Oh, you do like it, I know you do, that's why I have to do it," he would repeat, the awful hand going on stroking and probing in her.

And the terrible thing was that the hand did excite her, making her damp until she came—she didn't even know what was happening but she felt the great sickening release, when she would gasp, and he would say, "And now you must help me, please, Pussy Cat. You know your mother won't," pulling her head down into his lap. Afterward he would give her expensive presents, designer suitcases, fancy pens, bright beautiful scarves, and her mother would complain. Her only escape was school.

"Your mother didn't want perhaps to understand," Miss Martin says now.

"She did finally get Father to send me to boarding school," Diane says.

Miss Martin pushes her dark curls back from her face, and exclaims, "Oh, yes, boarding school! I'm sorry, with all this going on I forgot to tell you. I spoke to your headmistress. She sounded quite cross!"

"You did?" Diane says, abandoning the dishes and sitting down opposite Miss Martin, looking at her face with its red blotches and the dark curls which fall lankly about her cheeks, the dressing gown which is half open on her bony chest. "What did she say? What did *you* say?"

"I said that sometimes stealing can be a way of asking for help, that your mother had left so suddenly and unexpectedly and your father had up and married his secretary right away, that you are, after all, such an excellent student—one of her best and an asset to the school, obviously Ivy League material. That mollified her a bit. But she really changed her tune when I said your father and I were considering a gift to your excellent school—I sent quite a substantial check, actually."

"You did? What did Daddy say?" Diane asks, putting her hand to her lips.

"Oh—I didn't think it necessary to mention the conversation to him. I just said I thought it wise to be generous with your school. After all, your college applications are coming up soon, and you will need good references. That did the trick. He actually complimented me on my quick thinking and thanked me for watching out for you."

"Gosh!" Diane says, opening her eyes wide with admiration. Miss Martin, despite her red eyes and her greasy hair, despite the dishes, looks fascinating to Diane again. How did she manage to think of such a thing? she wonders.

Suddenly Diane feels glad to be sitting in the sunny kitchen at the old wooden table where her mother would cut up vegetables and where Diane would fill in the pictures in her coloring book. She feels hopeful as she did sometimes as a little girl looking out the window at the branches of the tall magnolia tree stirring in the breeze against the blue sky, thinking she has all the summer before her to enjoy the beach and the sea and that she will be able to go back to her school in the fall.

"Luckily, your father opened a joint account for us before we married, though I'm afraid now that . . ." and she begins to weep again.

Diane says, "I think I know how we could manage at least an afternoon off."

VI

Of course they do not expect him to try to jump. It is so easy to remove the ladder when he is up in the sleeping loft alone one afternoon, and then to grab their swimsuits and take off in Miss Martin's red Renault. Despite the woman's incompetence in the kitchen, she is a fast and excellent driver. They just drive down to the sea and go for a long swim—Miss Martin, it turns out, is a good swimmer. They swim out together leaving the shore behind, ducking under the big waves and then riding them back onto the shore.

Then they drive all the way to Montauk to Diane's favorite restaurant which looks over the sea, where they order clam chowder, lobster, and cheesecake, which they pay for with Diane's father's credit card while he is pacing up and down in the attic increasingly incensed.

When they arrive back, Diane's father has tried to jump down from the loft, which might have been possible without injury but he has fallen on the ladder which Diane left on the floor below. He is lying there making the sort of noises Diane remembers from the car. He has difficulty breathing. The doctors will later discover he has punctured a lung.

Miss Martin takes control of the situation as if she were his secretary again. She calls 911; then she speaks to Diane's father, leaning down to talk in his ear with her South African accent as he lies gasping on the floor. She says nothing about the ladder but tells him that in her opinion it might be wise not to antagonize his daughter in any way in the future, as she is a remarkably enterprising young woman (and indeed Diane's father does not bother her again and watches her warily at all times until she leaves for college).

Then Miss Martin shakes Diane's hand firmly, wishes her all the best, and takes off immediately in her car to go—Diane discovers later—to empty the joint account. Diane never sees her again, but she still thinks about her at times and considers that her father's initial estimation of her skills was correct: "Remembers everything, is utterly discreet, always there when you need her; never there when you don't."

Six Poems

by Margaret Atwood

Siren Brooding on Her Eggs

So many distant humans, wondering
what song we sang
to lure that many sailors
to their deaths, granted,

but what sort? Of death
I mean. Sharp birdclaws
in the groin, a rending pain, fanged
teeth in the neck? Or a last breath
exhaled in bliss, like that
of male praying mantises?

I sit here on my frowsy nest
of neckties, quarterly
reports, and jockey shorts
mixed in among the bones and pens,
and fluff my breasts and feathers. Lullaby,

my minimyths, my hungry little egglets,
dreaming in your glowing shells

of our failsafe girly secret.
Mama's right nearby
and Daddy must have loved you:
look—he gave you all his protein!

Hatching day's here. Be strong!
Soon I'll hear a tap-tap-tap, ahoy!
and out you'll break, my babies,
down-covered, pink and lovely,
flapping your tiny feathery wings,
and ravenous with song.

Thriller Suite

1.
Newsstands blow up
for no reason. Bookstores as well.
You're clamped to a windowsill
gibbering with adrenaline
as the light beam swings past you.
Holy hell, you whisper.
Those words are finally meaningful.

2.
The woman you were certain loved you
did not. Never did.
A puckered heart she had,
testicle on a plate
three days cold.
She used to cut your grapefruit for you,
have a Scotch waiting,
knives and poisons on her mind.
Now she's got sunglasses.
Who seduced her?

3.
Those girls manacled to the wall—
you laughed at them in old movies.
They used to wear torn jumpsuits.
You thought they were a prop.
But now they're everywhere,

naked from the waist down,
pink, black, bruise purple.

4.
Too many cars ruined,
festooned with red and gray.
Vein glue, brain jelly
all over the upholstery.
They'll never get the smell out,
whoever cleans up afterward.
It's an art.
Nobody sees that part.

5.
That older man in the suit,
the one with the briefcase,
the sneering one, with the shaved head—
you've seen him before.
Your stern, mean father
come back from the dead,
his neck a snarl of sutures.
He says *I told you not to.*
How waterproof are you?

6.
Everything's suddenly clearer,
though also more obscure.
You don't have to love anyone.
That eon's over.
But how free you feel!
How buoyant, as you're floating

from rooftop to rooftop,
leaking time from your many punctures
as the Glocks tick and tock.

7.
Behind you there's howling.
Ahead, an unturned corner.
There's fur on your nape. There's fear.
Wake up! Wake up!
In all these dreams, you're falling.

Passports

We save them, as we save those curls
culled from our kids' first haircuts, or from lovers
felled too early. Here are

all of mine, safe in a file, their corners
clipped, each page engraved
with trips I barely remember.

Why was I wandering from there to there
to there? God only knows.
And the procession of wraith's photos

claiming to prove that I was me:
the faces grayish disks, the fisheyes
trapped in the noonhour flashflare

with the sullen jacklit stare
of a woman who's just been arrested.
Sequenced, these pics are like a chart

of moon phases fading to blackout; or
like a mermaid doomed to appear onshore
every five years, and each time altered

to something a little more dead:
skin withering in the parching air,
marooned hair thinning as it dries,
cursed if she smiles or cries.

Spider Signatures

Hour by hour I sign myself—
a smear, a dot, a smear,
white semaphore on the black floor.

Spider shit.
What's left of the enticed.
Why is it white?
Because my heart is pure,
though I myself am ulterior,

especially under the bookcase:
a fine place for my silken pockets,
my wisps and filaments,
my looms, my precious cradles.

I've always liked books,
by preference paperbacks,
crumbling and flyspecked.
To their texts I add
my annotations, harsh and untidy:

moth wings, beetle husks, my own shed skins
like spindly gloves.
Apt simile: I'm mostly fingers.

I don't like the floor, though.
Too visible, I hunch, I scuttle,

a prey to shoes and vacuums,
not to mention whisks.

If you come across me suddenly
you scream: too many legs,
or is it the eight red eyes,
the glossy blob of abdomen?
Drop of thumb's blood, popped grape:
that's what you'd aim for.

Though it's bad luck to kill me.
Come to terms:
before you were, I am.
I arrange the rain,
I take hard care,

and while you sleep
I hover, the first grandmother.
I trap your nightmares in my net,
eat the seeds of your fears for you,
suck out their ink

and scribble on your windowsill
these tiny glosses on *Is, Is, Is,*
white lullabies.

Cassandra Declines the Gift

What if I didn't want all that—
what he prophesied I could do
while coming to no good
and making my name forever?
Dye my hair black, pierce my face,
spew out fuckshaped energy,
hook up, kick back.
Wallow in besmirching fame.

What if I said No Thank You
to Mr. Musician God,
to sex for favors?
What if I stayed right here?
Right in my narrowing hometown?
(Which will later be burned down.)
Thinking of others first
and being manless and pitiable?
I'd have a dark-blue leather purse,
and crochet cotton gifts
—dolls' hats, toilet-paper covers—
the nieces would throw out later.
Then I could cry about failure,
pale, sere, minor.

At least I would not be brazen,
like a shield maiden, like a fender.
At least I would not be brash

and last seen alive
that day in mid-November,
at the gas station, shivering, hitching,
in the dusk, just before

Update on Werewolves

In the old days, all werewolves were male.
They burst through their bluejean clothing
as well as their own split skins,
exposed themselves in parks,
howled at the moonshine.
Those things frat boys do.

Went too far with the pigtail yanking—
growled down into the pink and wriggling
females, who cried *Wee wee*
wee all the way to the bone.
Heck, it was only flirting,
plus a canid sense of fun:
see Jane run!

But now it's different:
no longer gender specific.
Now it's a global threat.

Long-legged women sprint through ravines
in furry warm-ups, a pack of kinky
models in sado *French Vogue* getups
and airbrushed short-term memories,
bent on no-penalties rampage.

Look at their red-rimmed paws!
Look at their gnashing eyeballs!

Look at the backlit gauze
of their full-moon subversive haloes!
Hairy all over, this belle dame,
and it's not a sweater.

O freedom, freedom and power!
they sing as they lope over bridges,
bums to the wind, ripping out throats
on footpaths, pissing off brokers.

Tomorrow they'll be back
in their middle-management black
and Jimmy Choos,
with hours they can't account for
and first dates' blood on the stairs.
They'll make some calls: *Goodbye.*
It isn't you, it's me. I can't say why.
They'll dream of sprouting tails
at sales meetings,
right in the audiovisuals.
They'll have addictive hangovers
and ruined nails.

Assassin

by Joyce Carol Oates

A*ssassin.* Hissing sound like snakes. First came to me through the steam radiator. Waking open-mouthed and the inside of my mouth raw and festering from what had been done to it while I'd been made to sleep a drugged sleep in this terrible place.

Then, the whisper of hope—*Assassin. Assassin!*

The room I was assigned at Saint Clement House, this was the first insult. This was unforgivable. The room, the bed, the bed with a lumpy smelly mattress, on a high floor of the House. Had to climb stairs. With my swollen ankles, weight. Panting like a dog. Had to make my way along the winding corridor like a rat in a maze. Insult at my age. *Pre-diabetic* was the diagnosis. *Hypertension.* To be assigned such sleeping quarters, in a bloody attic, low ceiling, no privacy, I would have to share a dreary dripping lavatory with strangers; it was not fair or just.

Saint Clement House where residents are the staff, and the staff are residents. You will look out for one another, they told us. Smug bastards all of them. There are (paid) nurses, nurses' aides, attendants, but not many of these, and so we are all obliged to assist one another (unpaid) when required. Dr. Shumacher is the resident psychologist but Dr. S. does not reside in the House and does not linger in the House any longer than is necessary for the bastard is clear of us by five p.m. and on his way. I was meant to be an equal of Dr. S. (for I am educated) but was cheated of my destiny by reason of my sex (female). Also, unacknowledged enemies in the government. After my discharge from the "hospital" where I was kept (against my volition) for eight months. Deemed not ready to return to a normal life and so sentenced to a *halfway house* as it is (laughably) called. *Half-arsed halfway-house* it is. And now, the worse insult, to be assigned one of the fifth-floor dormer rooms where at fifty-three I am old enough to be the grandmother of most of the residents. And I am not a junkie, or a souse. I am not gaga like some. I am not a filthy slut— hardly. But forced to cohabit with such crippled specimens of humanity for the sake of a bed and food to eat until I am well enough again to live by myself and tend to my own needs.

My only friend does not live here. My dear friend like a sister I have known since St. Agatha's grade school is Priss Reents who is my age and stout like me and with a plain, honest face like raw bread dough. When I am well enough again, Priss Reents has said I might live with her, in a room in her house if I could pay just a few dollars a week to help with rent and expenses. It is very surprising—Priss Reents is a cleaning woman for the PM himself, would you believe that?—yet it is so; for thirty years Priss Reents has worked for the same cleaning service that is assigned to the PM's residence at Queen's Square. But if you ask the woman what the PM is like, she will blink and stammer and seem not to know.

Guess I don't see much of him, or any of them.

A dull female, not like *me*.

Well, I'd known that Priss Reents cleaned the PM's residence and had done so for many years, but it never struck me much until the other day, waking like I did stunned and swallowing, not knowing at first where the hell I was. Hissing in the radiator—*Assassin.*

Love the sound of that word—*Assassin!*

Not *killer*—not *murderer.* Those are common words. Not even *executioner.* (Though there is something about this word that I am beginning to admire.)

Assassin. Executioner. In the service of fairness and justice.

The insult of my room on the fifth floor and how we are fed here in the *half-arsed halfway house.* Cold gluey oatmeal one morning, and when I spat out a mouthful onto my spoon, I was disgusted to see what resembled a small, wizened piece of meat.

Your own heart—the whisper came to me, laughing.

Yet, the idea of *assassination* did not occur to me for some time. I have lost track of the days since that time but it might have been a month at least. What began in the hissing, in a dream, and spread out of the dream, like a potato sprouting roots in dank soil—*Assassin.*

Somehow it came to me that I would saw off the head of the arrogant bastard PM. This would be my destiny, not the other—not to be Dr. S. and lord it over the mentally enfeebled, addicts, and sluts, for I'd been cheated of that career. But this, I would not be cheated of and would go down in history like the Hebrew Judith in her triumph over Holofernes.

Assassin. Assassin! I was slow to realize and to accept, as you would be if you won a lottery and did not dare to believe. *Have I—won? The winner is—me?*

Almost, I could hear the crowds applauding on the TV.

Hateful, arrogant son of a bitch the PM was, you saw clearly on TV. A bachelor he was—never married. No worse than any of them in any of the "political parties," but the PM is the top dog deserving of his bloody head sawed off. And fitting: the very person who scrubbed his filthy toilet should be the one to saw it off.

You see, no one notices us. This will be our revenge.

Short, squat, middle-aged female like Priss Reents/me moves through the world invisible. She/I have bunions, varicose veins, swollen ankles. She/I are short of breath making our way upstairs. Hell, we are short of breath making our way downstairs. Not five foot three, one hundred seventy pounds. No one has glanced at us in decades. Not a man or a boy in memory. We are as deserving of respect as any of you, yet we do not receive your bloody respect, so bloody hell with you.

In fact, this is our strength. An *assassin* in the figure of a middle-aged cleaning woman flush-faced and panting on the stairs, breasts like balloons collapsed to her waist, fattish thighs and buttocks in a nylon uniform—who'd suspect?

What, are you daft, man? That cow? That's the cleaning woman, for Christ's sake, man. Let'er through.

Something like this it was, that transpired that morning. Very cleverly I ground up a half-dozen sleeping pills to dissolve in Reents's coffee which the woman so dilutes with cream and sugar it is not even coffee any longer but some disgusting sugar concoction. And they are trying to say to me that I am the one who is *prediabetic*.

And so, there was no difficulty for me to put on Priss Reents's uniform when she was fast asleep and snoring with her vast mouth agape, and indeed the stretch-waist nylon trousers fit me like a fist in a glove. No difficulty for me to impersonate Priss Reents who is near enough to me to be a twin sister. So that even if a security guard had thought to actually look at me, he'd have seen Priss Reents and not me, for it was Priss Reents's ID photo pinned to my bosom slumping to my waist and he would not have even given that ID photo a second glance out of repugnance for that sort of female bosom. Also, Priss Reents wore an insipid knitted cap to disguise her thinning hair, which suited me too.

Okay, ma'am. Go on through.

If a man does glance at you, if you are Priss Reents/me, his eyes are glazed with boredom. Not for an instant does he *see*.

Waved through security without a hitch. Exactly as planned. Dragging a vacuum cleaner on wheels, mop and bucket, canvas bag in which were stuffed sundry cloths, brushes, and cleaning materials. From innocent queries posed to Priss Reents I had ascertained which corridor to take into the PM's private rooms, and there I swiftly left behind the cleaning items and sought out the bloody bastard in the swanky interior, for whom I was feeling a fierce hatred as if, in a dream of the night before, the PM had insulted me to my face as so many others have done. You would be as surprised as I was how swiftly I moved on my swollen ankles. Which would make me realize, in reflecting back over this episode, how the *assassination* was a foregone conclusion, like a final move in a chess game, except until just recently the *assassin* had not been named. And I would wonder if they had sought out others as the *assassin* in this case, and these others had proved inferior, and so they had settled upon me with the knowledge that I would not disappoint. For they must have known of me—my previous life, my education that had come to nothing, the sharpness of my intelligence blunted by myriad disappointments of which not a single one was my fault. In the man's bedroom, in his (black silk) stocking feet, there the

PM stood before a three-way mirror frowning as he buttoned a crisp-ironed white cotton dress shirt with his back to the door, unsuspecting, for Priss Reents would never have dared enter any room in the residence without knocking meekly beforehand, and if there was no knock, there could be no intrusion; if no intrusion by a stranger, there could be no sudden blow to the head from behind, so swift rushing into the penumbra of the mirror there was no chance for the targeted one to draw a breath, to escape the hard blow of a pewter urn selected from a mantel, fairly cracking the eggshell skull in that moment. *You will know what to do, as you do it*—the hissing voice had instructed out of the radiator, and so it was, in an adjoining kitchen there were fancy sharp knives on a magnet board, and of these I selected a knife with a double-serrated blade, and for the next half hour or more I was engaged in sawing off the head of the bloody PM as he lay helpless on the floor on a fancy thick-piled carpet. This "career politician" (as he was known) who had so many enemies in our country; any number of them would rejoice in my actions and thank me for my patriotism. To sever a (living) head from a (living) body is no easy task and it is very bloody and tiring, as you might imagine, but the PM was deeply unconscious from the blow to his skull and could put up little resistance.

The Head (as I would call it) was mine as soon as it was cleanly severed from the body. It was larger than you would think, and it was heavier. And very bloody, with veins and sinews and twitchy nerves dripping nonstop from the ragged neck. And the skin of the face was coarse and darkening, as with chagrin. And the eyes were half-shut, droopy-lidded like a drunkard's. And the hair which was thin, grizzled-gray, and not a handsome whitish silver such as you are accustomed to seeing on the PM in his public appearances—a hairpiece which (evidently) he would fix upon his head when he left his quarters.

"Missing your hairpiece, are you, love?"—the wisecrack issued from my lips, unbidden.

I wondered if this would be a new trait of mine: a co-quettish sort of wit. For it was very unlike my usual self in the presence of men, I can testify.

The Head was too stunned to respond. Of the eyes, the left had all but disappeared inside its socket while the right was trying very hard to fix me in focus, to determine what was what. For the PM had not gotten to his position in the government without being sharp-witted. Out of kindness as much as mischief, I sought out the hairpiece in an adjoining bathroom, and this I placed upon the near-bald scalp, and adjusted as best as I could, for even in his decapitated state the PM was something of a lady's man.

Almost you have to smile, to register a man's vanity at such a time.

Soon, then, I would exit the PM's chambers trailing vacuum cleaner, mop and bucket, canvas bag. And in the bag, wrapped in plastic to prevent the blood from soaking through, the Head. And a dollop of disinfectant to make the nostrils pinch.

Leaving the PM's residence, you are not scrutinized. There is only precaution against bringing a deadly instrument into the residence, and when you exit it is by a different door.

Still, it was early—not yet eight a.m. If they'd had their wits about them they might've wondered why the cleaning woman was leaving so early, but indeed they took no more notice of her than of a fly buzzing to be let out.

From Priss Reents I knew that the shiny black limousine

to bear the PM across town to the capitol building would not appear until eight thirty a.m. and so no one would miss the deceased until then.

The headless body I had left covered with a quilt from the disheveled bed. Being *headless,* a body is of not much interest and interchangeable with others of its sex, it seemed to me.

In Priss Reents's rubber-soled shoes, with Priss Reents's ID photo removed from my bosom, and a coarse-knit nylon cardigan of an unusual shade of lavender, that resembled nothing of Priss Reents's, and the insipid knitted cap removed, I took the Land's End trolley to the end of the line. There is a place here I know that I have not visited in years, but I'd once known well, down behind a boardwalk by the beach, in an area of the beach that is no longer much frequented, and here the Head would not be easily discovered. My plan was to bury it in the coarse damp sand with care, for this part of the *assassination* seemed to be left to me to devise; as it often happens, a know-it-all will instruct you what to do but neglect to include the complete instructions, so you must supply them yourself. Women are familiar with this; it was not surprising to me. The Head comprehended my plan, for the right eye was fixed upon me with alarm. Though luridly bloodshot, that eye was sharp-focused. *Don't abandon me*—it begged.

Such nonsense! I wasn't about to listen to such nonsense. In life the PM had had a wheedling way about him that was often remarked upon. A right proper bastard, the PM. One-quarter Scots blood, it was said of him. One of those sly ones who would *get his bloody way* if you were not careful.

So I hid the Head in a safe-keeping place behind a shuttered stall. Still in the canvas bag, but it was so grimy a bag, in the most desperate eyes not worth stealing. By this time

I was very hungry and so went out to have a snack on the boardwalk, then returned, and there inside the bag was the Head flush-faced and chagrined and the left eye adrift but the right eye blinking in the harsh oceanside light and accusing. *Don't abandon me. Please! Your secret is safe with me—I will not tell them what you've done.* And, most piteous—*Don't bury me like garbage, I beg you.*

The Head most feared being buried alive. I took pity on the Head, for I could understand how it felt in such circumstances.

In a few days I would come to a decision, I thought. In the meantime, the Head is doing no harm. We are in a sheltered place where there is no one to hear it, and it cannot escape (of course). I have set it on a platter, with some moisture beneath, to keep it moist, as you would keep a succulent plant moist, now that the bleeding has stopped, or mostly stopped. Atop the scalp I have affixed the silvery hairpiece, as the Head is anxious not to be seen without it.

The Head has quickly become a familiar presence. Like a husband of many years. (Once, I'd had a husband. I think I remember this. But not the actual man, and not myself as a wife, I don't remember.) *Please have pity on me. Please love me. Don't bury me*—the Head dares to whisper. And—*Kiss my lips! I love you. Please.*

But at this request, I just laugh. I will not *kiss your lips,* or anyone's bloody lips. I am calculating where to bury you, in fact. Farther out the pebbly shore but deep enough so the gulls don't smell you and dig you up and cause a ruckus. No, I am too smart for that. Fact is, I am just sitting here having a rest, and I am thinking, and when I am finished thinking I will know more clearly what to do, and I am not taking bloody orders from you, my man, or from any man ever again.

About the Contributors

Liam Sharp

MARGARET ATWOOD is the author of more than fifty books of fiction, poetry, and critical essays. In addition to *The Handmaid's Tale*, her novels include *Alias Grace*, which won the Giller Prize in Canada and the Premio Mondello in Italy; *The Blind Assassin*, winner of the Man Booker Prize; *Oryx and Crake*, a finalist for the Giller Prize and the Man Booker Prize; and her most recent, *The Heart Goes Last*. She lives in Toronto with the writer Graeme Gibson.

Max S. Gerber

AIMEE BENDER is the author of five books, including *The Girl in the Flammable Skirt*, a *New York Times* Notable Book, and *The Particular Sadness of Lemon Cake*, recipient of a SCIBA Book Award. Her short fiction has been published in *Granta*, *Harper's*, the *Paris Review*, and more, and heard on *This American Life* and *Selected Shorts*. She lives in Los Angeles, and teaches creative writing at USC.

Maria Kanevskaya

STEPH CHA is the author of *Follow Her Home*, *Beware Beware*, and *Dead Soon Enough*. Her fourth and latest novel is *Your House Will Pay*. She is the noir editor for the *Los Angeles Review of Books* and a regular contributor to the *Los Angeles Times* and *USA Today*. She lives in her native city of Los Angeles with her husband and two basset hounds.

Jonathan Demme

EDWIDGE DANTICAT is the author of several books, including *Breath, Eyes, Memory*, an Oprah's Book Club selection, and *Krik? Krak!*, a National Book Award finalist, as well as the novels-in-stories *The Dew Breaker* and *Claire of the Sea Light*. She is also the editor of *Haiti Noir*, *Haiti Noir 2: The Classics*, and *The Best American Essays 2011*. Her most recent book is *The Art of Death: Writing the Final Story*.

Laurel Hausler

LAUREL HAUSLER is a painter, sculptor, illustrator, and photographer from the DC area. Her work portrays dark and mysterious tableaux of the female experience in an uncertain world. For more information, visit www.laurelhausler.com.

CASSANDRA KHAW is a scriptwriter at Ubisoft Montreal. Her work can be found in *F&SF, Lightspeed, Tor.com*, and *Strange Horizons*. She has also contributed to titles such as *Sunless Skies, Fallen London, Wasteland 3,* and *She Remembered Caterpillars*. Her first novella, *Hammers on Bone*, was nominated for a Locus Award and the British Fantasy Award. Her most recent novel, *Food of the Gods*, was nominated for a Locus Award.

SHEILA KOHLER is the author of ten novels, three volumes of short fiction, and most recently a memoir, *Once We Were Sisters*. She has won two O. Henry prizes, and has been included in *The Best American Short Stories* twice. Her work has been published in thirteen countries, and she teaches at Columbia and Princeton. Her novel *Cracks* was made into a film directed by Jordan Scott, Ridley Scott's daughter.

LISA LIM is a comic storyteller born and raised in Queens, New York. Her graphic stories have been featured in *Guernica, PANK,* and *Mutha*. She is also the illustrator of a children's book called *Soma So Strange*. Her comics can be found at lisalimcomics.com.

LIVIA LLEWELLYN'S fiction has appeared in over forty anthologies and magazines and has been reprinted in multiple best-of anthologies, including *The Best Horror of the Year, Year's Best Weird Fiction,* and *The Mammoth Book of Best New Erotica*. Her short story collections *Engines of Desire: Tales of Love & Other Horrors* and *Furnace* were both nominated for the Shirley Jackson Award for Best Collection. You can find her online at liviallewellyn.com.

VALERIE MARTIN is the author of eleven novels, including *Trespass, Mary Reilly, Italian Fever,* and *Property*, four collections of short fiction, and a biography of St. Francis of Assisi. She has been awarded a grant from the National Endowment for the Arts and a John Simon Guggenheim Fellowship, as well as the Kafka Prize and an Orange Prize. Martin resides in Dutchess County, New York, and is currently a professor of English at Mount Holyoke College.

ELIZABETH MCCRACKEN is the author of six books, including *Bowlaway*, her most recent. She has received grants and awards from the Guggenheim Foundation, the American Academy in Berlin, and the Radcliffe Institute for Advanced Study, among other accolades. *Thunderstruck & Other Stories* won the 2015 Story Prize. She lives in Austin, Texas, with her husband, the writer and illustrator Edward Carey, and their children.

Edward Carey

BERNICE L. MCFADDEN is the author of nine critically acclaimed novels, including *Sugar, Gathering of Waters* (a *New York Times Book Review* Editors' Choice and one of the 100 Notable Books of 2012), *Glorious, The Book of Harlan* (winner of a 2017 American Book Award and the NAACP Image Award for Outstanding Literary Work, Fiction), and *Praise Song for the Butterflies*. She is a four-time Hurston/Wright Legacy Award finalist.

Makeda Miller

JENNIFER MORALES is a poet, fiction writer, and performance artist based in rural Wisconsin. Her story "Cousins" appeared in *Milwaukee Noir*. Her first book, *Meet Me Halfway*, a short story collection about life in hypersegregated Milwaukee, was the Wisconsin Center for the Book's 2016 Book of the Year. Morales is president of the board of the Driftless Writing Center in Viroqua, Wisconsin. For more information, visit www.moraleswrites.com.

Jennifer Morales

JOYCE CAROL OATES is the author of a number of works of fiction, poetry, and nonfiction. She is the editor of *New Jersey Noir* and *Prison Noir* and a recipient of the National Book Award, PEN America's Lifetime Achievement Award, the National Humanities Medal, and a World Fantasy Award for Short Fiction. She lives in Princeton, New Jersey, and was recently inducted into the American Philosophical Society.

Charles Gross

S.J. ROZAN is the author of fifteen novels, more than seventy-five short stories, and the editor of two anthologies, including *Bronx Noir*. She has won multiple prizes, such as the Edgar, Shamus, Anthony, Nero, and Macavity awards; the Japanese Maltese Falcon; and the Private Eye Writers of America Lifetime Achievement Award. Rozan was born in the Bronx and lives in lower Manhattan.

Iden Ford

Heather Laszlo

S.A. SOLOMON'S short stories and poems have been published in the anthologies _New Jersey Noir, Jewish Noir, Skin & Bones, 55 Stories to Benefit Protect: Protectors 2: Heroes,_ and _Grand Central Noir._ Her work has also appeared in _Down & Out: The Magazine, Mondays Are Murder, Shotgun Honey,_ and _The Five-Two._ She is a member of the New York chapter of the Mystery Writers of America.

Claudia Royal Coleman

LUCY TAYLOR'S work has most recently appeared in the collection _Spree and Other Stories_ and in the anthologies _Endless Apocalypse, The Beauty of Death II: Death by Water, Monsters of Any Kind,_ and _Tales from the Lake Volume 5._ Taylor's novelette _Sweetlings_ was on the final ballot for the 2017 Bram Stoker Awards in the category of nonfiction. Her Stoker Award–winning novel, _The Safety of Unknown Cities,_ is being published in German by Festa Verlag.

Made in the USA
Coppell, TX
17 November 2021

65944812R00152